Reignite

J.M. DARHOWER

Reignite is a work of fiction. Names, characters, places and incidents are the products of the author's imagination or are used fictitiously. Any resemblance to actual events, locals, or persons, living or dead, is entirely coincidental.

To my mama, who shines brightly above, a twinkling star in the vibrant night sky. I miss you more than words can say.

"One must pay dearly for immortality. One has to die several times while still alive." – Friedrich Nietzsche

Contents

ℜrologue

Puffs of smoke wisped from the smoldering blade as the tip of the sword dragged against the marble floor. Michael strolled through the chamber, his bare feet heavy, his head held low.

He paused when he reached the front, his gaze slowly lifting toward the massive Victorian throne. It matched the rest of the room—all burgundy velvet and shimmering gold.

His eyes met his Father's, crystal clear and blue as day. He seemed at ease, slouched slightly, His eternally youthful face expressionless. Michael regarded Him with caution, unable to detect any hints of emotion. It wasn't unusual... He never gave himself away. But today, of all days, Michael hoped to find something, some indication of what would happen next.

Michael opened his mouth to speak, but no words came out. It was pointless to try to explain it, anyway. Their Father saw all and knew all. He'd watched everything play out.

A moment passed, then another of strained silence, before He finally spoke. "You did well today."

Michael gaped at Him. "I spared a miscreant."

"You showed great compassion."

"Satan is still out there..."

"No, he's not. The dragon has been slayed."

Confusion crept through Michael. How could that be? He'd healed Serah, sparing her from eternal damnation in a split second decision fueled by weakness and lingering love, and he had been summoned straight to their Father the moment it was complete. He'd left Satan sitting in the middle of the deserted street, still holding Serah in his arms, the two covered in filth.

Michael hadn't had a chance to slay him.

"I don't understand."

"I know you don't, son."

Slowly, He raised his hand, swiping it through the air. Michael felt a rush of energy pass through him as his Father oh-so-easily cleaned up the bloody mess. The sun would shine again, the flowers would bloom, and life would go back to how it had been before.

Except... now he didn't have Serah in his life.

"I've only ever tried to obey you, Father. I only wanted to fulfill my destiny."

"Your destiny wasn't to *kill* him, Michael," He said quietly. "That was never my intention. In fact, I'm not even certain you could. There's a reason he's the one who originally sat beside my throne."

Those words cut Michael deep, striking a simmering human emotion somewhere inside of him. *Jealousy.*

"I just wanted the hatred inside of him—the pride, the anger, the arrogance—to finally go away."

His Father motioned toward the chair beside the throne. Michael instinctively dropped his sword, the metal clattering against the floor, as he wearily stepped over and plopped down. It had been his seat for the past six thousand years, day after day, night after night, but he still felt like he was merely keeping it warm for somebody else. He still lived in Lucifer's shadow, judged by Satan's countless sins.

"And has it?" Michael asked. "Has his hatred gone away?"

His Father tilted His head to the side. "I'm not sure."

Michael gaped at Him. Not sure? He was infallible. He knew everything. How could He not be sure about something like this?

His Father swiped his hand in the air again. This time the room before them vanished, the deserted street of Chorizon coming into view. It was so clear, so close, that it was as if nothing but a thin glass wall separated them.

"Your brother is a peculiar one."

"My brother?"

"Yes. Lucifer."

Brother. The word brought Michael nothing but heartache. His brother was dead. Wasn't he?

"Just look at him," He continued. "He's stripped bare, and it's hard to know what he'll become when he builds himself back up. But for now he sits there, cradling her in his arms—so protective, yet utterly defenseless. He knows, when she wakes, she won't remember him, yet he doesn't leave, because he loves her so much."

Michael's voice was a whisper. "I loved her, too."

"You did, son. And a part of her loved you. But there's a reason those two were given the same name."

Morning Star.

"What happens now?" Michael asked, staring at the projected image. Lucifer sat in total silence, clinging to Serah as she started to stir. "Should I return him back below? Imprison him once again?"

"No, I don't think that'll be necessary," He said. "Let him be."

Michael was flabbergasted. Let him be?

"Yes," his Father said, hearing Michael's thoughts, sensing his doubt. "Let's see what he does now that he's free again."

One

The massive forsaken castle was overrun with evil.

Demons had flocked to it in droves after the apocalypse came to an abrupt halt, descending upon the last place on Earth where Lucifer had made himself at home. They considered it base and gathered there, waiting on word from their leader. He wasn't in Hell, they thought, so where could he be?

The Dark Legion, they called themselves. *Fucking absurd.* They looked more like a hoard of bumbling idiots, mindless, hideous drones just sitting around and twiddling their thumbs like the worthless fucks they were.

Luce wasn't sure whether to be flattered or frustrated. The vilest creatures to walk the Earth seemed to be completely lost without his guidance. Had Lire been around, he would've had them organized, like a real army, instead of the frantic scene he encountered when he arrived there.

Too bad Lire met tragedy, going poof on the end of Michael's sword. Luce almost regretted not protecting the powerful demon more. *Almost.*

It would've saved him *this* headache, that's for certain.

Luce strolled into the old castle. The demons immediately shifted out of his way, the crowd parting like he was Moses and they were the Red Sea.

He wished he could drown them all, the pathetic excuse for an army.

Luce always demanded they come to him in human form, but most now stood around with their true nature exposed, their eerie ugliness displayed for all to see. *How easily they forget themselves.*

"My Lord," a demon said, one of the few that looked like a mortal, the lone soul brave enough to step into his path and address him. *Brave, or is it stupid?* The demon bowed his head out of respect. "Welcome back."

Luce pushed past the creature, not bothering with a response, as he made his way straight through to the golden throne. He plopped down on the seat, glaring, eyes taking in the sea of monsters, as he motioned toward the large double doors. "Get out."

They didn't waver, pushing and shoving to get out of the room, not wanting to face the wrath they could hear in his voice. The creature that had addressed him lingered, eyeing Luce curiously, as he took a few hesitant steps away.

"You," Lucifer said, pointing at him. "What do they call you?"

"Volac," the demon said.

"You take Lire's post while he's on sabbatical," Luce said. "Keep the others out of my hair, and inform me when Michael closes in."

"Yes, My Lord," the demon said, bowing. "Anything you wish."

Luce waved him away. "Now go."

He sat there, trying to hold everything inside, as he waited for the castle to clear out, for the creatures to take leave, before exploding. Energy purged from him in waves, the ground shaking like an earthquake struck, the sheer force of it enough to blow out what was left of the old stained glass windows. The glass shattered into millions of tiny fragments, sending them flying for miles like jagged bullets, slicing and dicing everything they struck. Blackness overtook the castle, the sky above a mass of dark clouds, lightning flashing as rain pelted the earth around it, incited by his bitter rage.

Luce's eyes stung.

He once told Serah he could cry, but that he

didn't. After all, what would Satan have to cry about? *Nothing*.

But nobody ever said he was honest.

No matter how hard he fought it back, tears fell from his eyes, the bitter, salty wetness staining his cheeks, fueling his aggression. This was how it had to go—she was a sacrifice he had to make, collateral damage in his quest for retaliation—but this wasn't how it was supposed to end.

He wasn't supposed to lose it all.

She wasn't supposed to mean so much to him.

Luce destroyed the castle in his rampage, bringing the medieval structure to its knees, as the other towers toppled around it like dominos. Built for a king, but it was no match for the King of Hell when he unleashed the beast. It crumpled, the stone turning to dust, blown away by the hurricane-force winds his fury stirred up.

He didn't stop there.

The ground around it was annihilated as if ravished by tornado, trees uprooted, life ruined. He would bring down half the world if it meant eradicating these feelings. He hopped from place to place, destroying, desolating, and pummeling towns to nothing before moving on to the next. Over and over, it went on for hours, one day morphing into the next. He apparated back to the remote area deep in the middle of Europe around dawn, the same place his rampage started, where the castle once stood.

Or rather, where the castle *still* stood.

The structure was back in place, tall and sturdy, exactly as it had been before he demolished it. Even the stained glass was once more in tact. He glared at it, his tears long ago dried up, his rage waning to exhaustion.

His Father was cleaning up his messes again.

Everything he harmed, everything he *killed* was brought right back to life, healed and fixed as if he hadn't tainted it. As if he hadn't touched it.

Everything except for *her*.

The world reset, the slate wiped clean again and again, but Serah was still gone, lost to him.

"Why?" he screamed, so loud everything around him shook again. "What do you want from me?"

An orange glow swaddled the land with warmth and brightness as the sun started to rise. As Luce's voice echoed through the sky, flowers popped up through the grass around him, blooming as if to send a message. The pinkish-purple stalks blanketed the land, a peculiar unpleasant odor filling the air.

Grimacing, Luce reached down and yanked a stalk from the ground. *Cleome serrulata*. Spider Flower. The last time he saw one, Serah had brought it with her to the gate and held it through the barrier for him. It had been the first time he touched her, the first time he felt that tingle beneath his skin, the tightening of his chest that he knew she felt, too.

The memory of that afternoon struck him hard, worming its way through his skull no matter how hard he tried to forget it, his own words haunting him. He couldn't escape it.

"Our Father offered more freedom to it than he did us," he told her, staring at the devious plant through the gate. *"This thing does what it wants with no regard, grows where flowers aren't supposed to grow, takes over fields and smothers everything else that lives there, killing it, and yet it's hailed as one of His magnificent creations. A fucking plant is given more leniency than me."*

"A plant doesn't think," she said. *"It doesn't make conscious decisions."*

"And what about mortals? His beloved humans, His favorite creation. He absolves them for everything as long as they ask. Why wasn't I shown that same mercy? I wasn't even given the chance to apologize."

Serah gaped at him. "Would you have apologized?"

22

"No. I did nothing wrong."

Luce laughed bitterly to himself, clenching his hand into a fist, crushing the flower before throwing it to the ground.

Message received.

But if God were waiting for an apology, he'd be waiting a long fucking time.

Countless colorful lights bounced off the Red Sea at night, surrounding the city of Eilat like a vibrant rainbow. Luce stood along the shoreline, staring out at the darkness, watching as the streaks of color rippled and swayed in the waves. The cool water lapped at his bare feet in regular intervals, receding before rushing back at him, over and over again.

He savored the sensation as he dug his toes into the wet sand, reminiscing of a time, not long ago, when the water before him boiled, a sea of bloody sludge he'd single-handedly brewed.

It had only been a few days time, yet every trace of his presence—every trace of the Great Battle that had taken place in the sacred land around him—had already been erased. Removed from existence, and from the minds of the people who lived and worked along these shores. They all forgot, already, while Luce remained cursed to remember every bit of it.

Every sordid detail, every single mistake, every second of heartache had been embedded in his brain, as crisp and clear as the moment it happened. The chaos he'd been accustomed to the past six thousand years—the cries for mercy, the screams of agonizing pain that constantly tried to force itself out of the confinement within his skull—was replaced with something else now: absolute silence.

There was no one, and nothing, to keep him company except for his nagging memories. He was still plugged into the Angel Network, but they knew he was listening now. The angels purposely blocked him from their thoughts, silenced their chatter to keep him in the dark, whispering occasionally in code so he wouldn't understand.

Blah blah fucking blah... nothing but bullshit.

It never ended.

Luce thought it was what he'd wanted—the silence, the peace—but what he hadn't anticipated was the loneliness. Nobody had bothered him, nobody had come for him, nobody even seemed to be concerned about him.

Why?

A loud pop of static electricity rocked the air behind him as he considered that. Luce tensed, expecting the pungent odor of his brother to assault his senses, like maybe he'd conjured him up, but instead a peculiar spicy scent wafted around him.

Whiskey and cigar smoke?

"Well, I'll be damned," a vaguely familiar voice spoke, low and gritty, with the hint of a Scottish accent.

Luce smiled to himself in recognition. "You almost were damned."

"Almost," he agreed. "Unlike you, though, I came to my senses."

"No, unlike me, you lost your fucking nerve."

Hearty laughter rang out. "Touché, my friend."

Friend.

Luce turned around, looking away from the glistening water, and glanced at his old friend for the first time in ages. "Abaddon."

Abaddon stood tall, dressed in a crisp blue suit, his bright white wings shimmering in the darkness. There was sharpness about him, his jawline chiseled, his nose pointy, his eyebrow cocked condescendingly.

His expression seemed harsh, but amusement danced in his light blue eyes, a stark contrast to his olive skin and long jet-black hair, pulled back at the nape.

"Luce," he said. "That was quite an entrance you made, nearly destroying the planet when you waltzed in. The guys upstairs had their panties in a twist. They seemed to think for a moment you might succeed."

"I bet," Luce said. "But in my defense, well... never mind. Fuck it. I have no defense."

And no apologies, either.

Abaddon laughed. "You never did."

Comfortable silence settled around them for a moment before Luce let out a deep sigh. "The big guy send you?"

Abaddon shook his head. "Nope. Just had to see you with my own eyes."

Luce threw his hands up and motioned toward himself. "Well, get a good look, because it's only a matter of time before I'm gone again."

Truthfully, Luce was surprised he was still standing on the surface. After Michael had spared Serah, he'd expected his brother to cast him right back into the pit. He wouldn't have fought it—fighting was senseless. Luce had thrown his last card and lost the final game.

But instead of banishing him—instead of

punishing him—Michael had simply left. A second before he vanished, a telltale sparkling glow had surrounded him, enveloping him, sweeping him away. It was something Luce knew no one else could've seen, not even the other low-level winged bastards like Abaddon, but enough Archangel lingered in him to detect it. He'd even felt it briefly, the prickly sensation on his skin.

Their Father had summoned Michael.

And ever since his tantrum afterward, Luce had merely been wandering around the Earth, bouncing from place to place as he waited for Michael to reappear to finish what they'd started.

"Nah, you aren't going anywhere," Abaddon said. "It's not like you have anywhere to go, right?"

"Right." Luce drew out the word, eyeing the angel strangely. He could detect a hint of confusion in his voice. He knew when somebody was prying for information. You can't con a conman. "Don't bullshit me, Don. Why are you really here?"

Casually, Abaddon shrugged a shoulder. "Curiosity."

"About what?"

A fraction of a second hesitation. "About why you gave up so easily."

There it was.

Luce gazed at his old friend as that question sunk in. He hadn't said it, but Luce knew what he really meant by those words. "You want to know if the rumors are true."

Despite the angels trying to keep silent, some of their whispers managed to seep through. He heard the gossip. Notorious Lucifer, King of Hell, claimed to know love again.

Unfathomable.

"So?" Abaddon asked. "Did someone actually tame the Beast?"

Luce laughed bitterly, turning away from the nosey angel to look back out at the water. "Why does it matter?"

"Because it's you." Abaddon was at his side in the blink of an eye, staring at him. "You're the warrior, the rebel, the one who's brave enough to fight this archaic system without regret. We still believe in you. We're—"

"*Cowards,*" Luce said, cutting him off. "You're fucking cowards. That's all you are."

Long ago, before he'd been cast into the pit, before he lost everything that meant something to him, Luce had built quite the following, an alliance of rebel angels who believed in his cause. His army had been strong, formidable, so much so that he believed he was guaranteed success.

That was, until push came to shove, and half of those on his side withdrew from battle. They surrendered, pleading for mercy, and were granted forgiveness. Abaddon had not only been Luce's second in command, but he'd been his closest friend, and his deflection was something Luce never really came to terms with.

He'd abandoned him when things got tough.

If Luce had to rank the worst moments of his existence, Abaddon's betrayal would be up there with the day he was cast into the pit by his own brother.

Neither came close to the sting of losing Serah, though.

"The time wasn't right," Abaddon said, trying to defend himself. "We were destined to lose."

"What makes it so different now?"

"You have incentive."

"And I didn't then?"

"You wanted it then, but you need it now. Before it was about fighting for what we thought was fair… now it's about getting revenge for how you were wronged."

Anger rose inside of Luce, simmering in his gut. He turned to Abaddon, expression darkening. "You know nothing about how I've been wronged."

Abaddon took a step back, raising his hands defensively. "You're right. I can only imagine, and I'm sure my greatest nightmare isn't even a fraction of the reality. Which is why we thought for sure you were going to win. Even *they* thought you were going to win. But then you just backed down, you retreated... *why*?"

Closing his eyes, the moment played out before him—the moment Serah lost her Grace. "I had what I wanted."

"Her?" Abaddon asked. "The Power? Serah? Pardon me if I'm wrong, but you don't really have her now, do you? Yet another thing they've *taken* from you."

His voice had a note of incredulity to it that only made Luce's anger simmer more. He hadn't meant her at all. He meant he'd gotten his revenge, had gotten his taste of freedom, but hearing her name from Abaddon's lips stirred up his resentment. "I gave her up. There's a difference."

Abaddon slapped him on the back as he shook his head. "You keep telling yourself that, pal."

Luce said nothing in response, staring out at the colorful water again, trying to harness some of the tranquility to soothe him, but it was pointless. He couldn't absorb any light when so much of him was still consumed by the darkness.

Abaddon must've taken his silence to mean the end of the conversation, because he let out an exaggerated sigh and turned around, starting to walk away. After a few steps, he stalled. "We still believe, Lucifer. This world should be ours, not theirs. If you decide to fight for what has been stolen from you… if you decide to take a stand… I'm sure you'll figure out where to find me."

With a pop, he was gone, disappearing into the atmosphere, leaving Luce once more to his silence… once more to his loneliness.

"Name?"

"Sarah… I think."

"Last name?"

Serah shrugged. Did she even have one of those?

"Date of birth?"

"I'm not sure."

The man looked up from his decrepit computer and peered at her through a pair of thick, steel-rimmed glasses perched low on his nose. Skepticism marked his pudgy face. "You look like you're in your early 20's. What's your education? High school? College?"

"I have no idea."

He sighed exaggeratedly as he leaned back in his creaky, swiveling office chair. The small cubicle, hardly the size of a walk-in closet, was filled with stacks upon stacks of paperwork. "Let me see if I got this straight: you have no birth certificate, no social security number, no identification at all; you aren't even entirely sure of your name; you have no previous address, no current address, and no means to procure an address; you have zero education, zero references, and zero experience. Yet, you expect me to find you a job today?"

Serah nodded. "Yes."

It sounded about right to her.

He stared at her with disbelief for a moment before sitting back up, his gaze returning to his computer screen. "I'll see what I can do."

Serah shifted around on the uncomfortable little gray chair as she watched him type away at his keyboard. Something about the short balding man with the high-waist brown trousers charmed her the moment she'd stepped inside the Chorizon

Employment Commission, so much so that she'd sat around all afternoon, refusing to be seen by anybody else, as she waited for him to be available to help her. A strange sense of intuition, deep inside of her, told her he was the one to speak to about a job.

"Do you have any special skills?"

"Not that I know about."

"Can you type?"

"I suppose I could try."

"Have you ever driven a car?"

A light laugh tickled her chest, unexpected and inexplicable. "Yes, although I don't remember when, or where, or how, but I'm certain I have driven before."

He typed away for a moment longer as Serah studied his small wooden desk, cluttered with office supplies, his faded nameplate bearing the name Douglas Barnhart. Frustrated groans echoed from him after a while as he gave up on the computer and turned his attention back to her. He stared her down, eyes narrowed as if he were reading her.

"Look, miss, this office can't help you."

"But?" She knew there had to be a 'but'. She could hear it in his voice.

"But I might be able to do something."

Serah smiled radiantly as she jumped up from the chair and leaned across the desk, startling the man as she squeezed him in a hug. "Thank you so much, Mr. Barnhart."

"Whoa, wait, don't you want to hear what it is before you celebrate?"

"Oh." She sat back down. "Yes, of course."

"My mother owns this little place across town, the Barnhart Motel. She mentioned hiring some extra help. It's not glamorous, you know... will mainly be cleaning rooms and stuff like that. And while it won't pay much, I think I can get you somewhere to stay out of the deal."

"That sounds wonderful!"

"Yeah?"

"Absolutely."

He nodded as he grabbed his phone. "I'll set it up right now."

She watched him, satisfaction settling through her. She knew he would help her. Somehow, she knew.

Seven of clubs.
Ten of hearts.

Two of spades.

King of clubs.

Six of hearts.

Six of diamonds.

Six of spades.

Luce laughed bitterly to himself, staring at the dingy cards spread out on the asphalt beside him. He sat around the side of Chorizon Elementary School, leaning back against the brick wall facing the vacant playground.

Six. Six. Six. *What a fucking joke.*

He tossed down the rest of the deck, discarding the cards. It was useless. There was no point to the game with no one to play it with him.

But what else was there to do?

He had wandered for weeks, alone and utterly bored, somehow ending up right back here where it all had started. It was not far from the gates... so close, in fact, that Luce could feel the powerful energy emanating from them. It was a pulse in the air that reached out to him, tempting him back to familiar territory.

He'd be lying if he said he hadn't considered it. He was ten times stronger now that he was no longer marked, no longer cursed and confined by the magic.

He could voluntarily waltz right back through the gates, back into the darkened pit, and pick up where he'd left off, making life Hell for everyone around him.

Literally.

But something stopped him. Something stalled him, keeping him up top and lingering around this little town.

As soon as the thought passed through his mind, he caught a subtle whiff of a familiar scent and felt a spark of energy in the air around him. His eyes studiously scanned the playground and the surrounding streets until he spotted her.

Serah.

She was different now, with her flushed cheeks and heartbeat so strong he could hear it where he sat, but remnants of the angel still lingered in her body. Her essence was intact, calling out to him, somehow connecting with a part of his soul so strongly that he could almost feel her heart beating within his own chest.

Probably because you hijacked her Grace, asshole.

Remaining still, sitting on the filthy ground, Luce watched her in silence. She was casually strolling down the street, enjoying the afternoon sunshine.

Happiness surrounded her like a warm glow, a fact that made Luce both smile and viciously ache.

Guess ignorance really is bliss.

She paused near the community center, her brow slightly furrowing as she glanced around. She was looking for something, but what, Luce didn't know.

He couldn't hear her thoughts.

He sensed the connection with her, though. The residual angel in her recognized something in the air. Luce could tell from the way the glow surrounding her flared, like a spark igniting.

As he stared at Serah, desperately trying to get a read on her blank mind, a pop of static electricity echoed through the playground. He forced his gaze that direction, caught off guard by the sudden presence of another angel, seeing a female in a red dress with curly blonde hair. A Virtue, one of the nature dwellers. She stood a mere few feet from him, her gaze focused across the street at Serah.

The angel shielded her mind, her thoughts purposely blocked from Luce. He prodded, his protectiveness urging him to try to get some idea of her task, to figure out what the hell she wanted from Serah, to no avail.

The angel's attention shifted to him when she felt

him prying into her mind, her eyes narrowed. "You can't steal my thoughts, Satan."

Satan. Man, he still hated that fucking name. "Nice to see you, too."

"Nice?" she sneered, hostility in her voice he was unaware her kind was capable of possessing. "There is nothing nice about your existence. Your presence poisons the air, tainting everything I vow to protect."

He stared at her. *Dramatic much?*

"You, snake, are Earth's greatest enemy," she continued. "You're an abomination. A *mistake.*"

He cocked an eyebrow at her. "Thought Daddy didn't make mistakes."

She stepped toward him, glaring. Man, she was pissed. "You lack compassion, lack remorse. You may be free at the moment, but it won't last forever, because I'll make sure you pay for what you've done."

Through her anger, her guard slipped, letting Luce glimpse into her unbridled thoughts. Hannah was her name. Serah had been by her side since the beginning of time, and she harbored deep resentment over losing her best friend.

"Careful, Hannah," Luce said quietly, looking away from her. "Your wrath is showing."

Without responding, Hannah evaporated, the pop

of static loud. Luce glanced back at the street then, finding Serah long gone. Sighing, he gathered his cards and slipped them in his pocket for safekeeping before standing up and walking away from the school, determined to find her.

Serah had turned her attention away from the area and strolled down the street. Luce followed behind, hands needlessly shoved in the pockets of his black pants, bare feet dragging against the concrete.

He had no purpose for following her, other than driving himself crazy. Maybe he still got his rocks off on suffering, because seeing her and not being able to talk to her, or be with her, was undoubtedly torture of the worst kind. A few times he thought about touching her. She wouldn't feel it, or really know what it was she felt, the touch of an angel little more than a tickle, resonating deep inside of them, but he'd feel it.

And if he touched her, he suspected he wouldn't be able to let her go. He hadn't been brave enough to even get close enough to make that happen.

Maybe he was the coward now.

He followed her all day as she walked to and fro. He could hear some of the thoughts of those encountered, hear their assessment of the young woman who always smiled and never seemed to be in a hurry to get anywhere.

They thought it was weird, how she stopped to smell the flowers when she encountered some.

Luce thought there was nothing more beautiful.

Serah tugged at the stiff black dress as she gazed in the mirror, casually fixing the white apron tied around her waist. It was a stark contrast, the black and the white, the light and the dark against her pale skin.

It's not all black and white.

The peculiar words echoed through her mind, whispered in a voice that wasn't hers. She wasn't sure where they came from, or what they meant, but the words washed through her like they were gospel.

The room was cramped, barely large enough to contain the old double bed. It had a bathroom, though, and a small television, and even had a mini-fridge wedged into the corner. It was air conditioned and heated, and wired with electricity, giving Serah nearly everything she needed.

It wasn't perfect, but she wouldn't dare complain. She had a job and a place to stay, two things she had woken up without. The time following her injury, the mysterious incident that caused her memory to be wiped, had been filled with doctors and sterile hospital rooms, flimsy backless gowns and rehabilitation centers. They poked and prodded, interrogated and investigated, before merely shoving her out into the streets and wishing her the best of luck.

Compared to *that*? This was practically Heaven.

"Knock, knock."

Serah glanced toward the open doorway as Gilda Barnhart stepped into the room. She seemed a lot like her son, round and kind, with hair bordering between blonde and white.

"Hello," Serah greeted her, smiling warmly.

"I see the uniform fits."

Smoothing the material, Serah glanced down at herself. "It certainly does."

"So I brought your cart up and left it out on the walkway," Gilda said. "There are only two rooms occupied today, 7A and 21B. You'll want to talk to the front desk in the mornings for a list of our occupancies, just so you're aware, but your key is universal."

Serah pulled the key she'd been given when hired

from her dress pocket. It was a card that when swiped would open every door in the motel. She gazed at it, running her fingertips along the magnetic strip. "Thank you."

"Of course," she replied. "It's great to have you on board."

"It's great to be here," Serah said, meaning that as she said it.

Gilda gave her a quick rundown of what to do, which added up to basic maid services, nothing Serah couldn't handle. The woman departed with a whispered *good luck*, leaving Serah to her duties.

Neither rented room was actually occupied when Serah made it to them. She swiftly cleaned both, in and out and finished within an hour. She returned to the lobby of the motel and stepped inside, approaching Gilda as the woman sat behind the front desk.

"Now what?" she asked.

"Nothing," Gilda said. "That's it."

That was it? Didn't seem like much of a job to Serah. People worked from nine to five, didn't they? It was barely ten o'clock in the morning. "Are you sure?"

"Positive," Gilda said. "Enjoy the rest of your day."

Shrugging, Serah stepped back out of the lobby, on her way back to her room, when something across the street caught her eye. Her footsteps briefly faltered. It was a man, wearing all black, with dark hair, shorter on the sides and dramatic. He was handsome in a harsh way, his features sharp, his expression stoic like a hardened warrior, but that wasn't what stalled her.

What stalled her was the spark of recognition.

She'd seen him before.

And he was watching her.

There was something strange about him, the way he stood so still it was like he wasn't breathing, a fixture along the street, alive like the trees, but not swaying in the breeze. She recalled his face, a face she'd seen before, staring down at her when she awoke in the street, her mind a blank slate. No name, no identity, no sense of direction, but his eyes were as familiar as looking at her own reflection.

Her lips parted as she tried to think of his name. She knew it... she could feel it... but she couldn't think of it, no matter how hard she tried. She blinked rapidly, trying to force it forward by sheer will, but it evaded her.

As did he.

Another glance across the street and the man was gone, like he'd vanished into thin air.

Sin.

It was *everywhere*.

Greed. Wrath. Sloth. Pride. Envy. Gluttony. Lust.

Luce could feel it permeating the air like a fog, growing denser as he approached the bar on the outskirts of the city. The place appeared rundown, like the remnants of a long ago abandoned saloon, the old porch falling apart, the windows broken, but people still frequented it.

Sinners.

It wasn't a place anyone with a stitch of self-respect would step foot into, so it didn't surprise Luce a bit that Abaddon's essence was all over it. While angels couldn't technically feel, the emotions of uninhibited humans tended to have an affect on the guardians. The sins were raw, pure power in the air, which called to them like an emergency beacon, feeding their energy.

The more depravity, the stronger the Guardians.

Luce could feel the humans because he'd been damned, fallen from Heaven, tapped into the sensations, but Abaddon was the closest to mortal as angels got. Humans often depicted Guardian Angels as lifesavers, guides that existed to keep them safe, but more often than not, Guardians were dicks, spending their days mingling with humans and mocking their mistakes. And they certainly weren't the beautiful beings all the paintings portrayed them as.

Abaddon, for instance, looked like a fucking pirate that hadn't bothered to bathe in weeks.

Luce lingered outside the bar for a moment, absorbing the unsavory sensations, before strolling inside. His gaze was immediately drawn to Abaddon, sitting casually on top of the very end of the bar and leaning back against the wall, his wings fully emerged.

Flashy son of a bitch.

Nobody saw him.

Nobody knew he was there.

He looked up as Luce approached, a sly smile twisting his lips. "Well, well, well... if it isn't the Prince of Darkness."

Luce slid onto the stool right in front of him, refusing to respond to the title. It was almost as bad as Satan. "Don."

"What brings you by?"

Truth be told, Luce didn't know. He was just

tired of wandering all alone. "Was just in the neighborhood."

Abaddon laughed. "Can't say an Archangel has ever dropped by these parts before."

"Yeah, well, I don't know that I count," Luce said. "I'm more of a hybrid these days."

Curiosity twinkled in Abaddon's eyes. "You still got your wings, right?"

"Yes."

"Then you count."

Luce didn't agree, but he didn't argue. Archangels were holy, and Luce had drifted about as far from that as possible. He fit in more here with these ingrates than he did with the divine winged type.

A woman strolled by them, slipping onto the stool right beside Luce, absently waving for the bartender. She ordered shots of Tequila for her and her friends, and sat there, drumming her long pink fingernails on the bar as she waited. Her platinum blonde hair was teased, her black dress tight and short, low cut on her chest.

Lust coated her like a perfume.

Abaddon remained in his spot on the bar, his gaze fixed right on the woman's breasts as they bounced and jiggled whenever she moved. Luce shook his head at the angel's obvious ogling, and didn't need to tap into his thoughts to know what his old friend was thinking.

"So how do you do it?" Luce asked, raising an eyebrow in question.

"Do what?" Abaddon asked without even looking at him.

"Keep your Grace," Luce said. "Your mind is as corrupted as everyone else in this room."

"Ah, I think it, but I don't act on it," Abaddon said, turning to him when the woman got up and sauntered off with her alcohol. "My thoughts may be impure, but I own it, and resist temptation, so He forgives my wicked ways."

"That's not how it works."

"If we confess our sins, He is faithful and just and will forgive us our sins and purify us from all unrighteousness," Abaddon said, his voice monotone as he quoted scripture. "Maybe you need to brush up on your Bible, pal."

An inkling of anger tickled Luce's spine. "I don't need to read it. I *lived* it. Forgiveness is for them, not us."

"You're wrong," Abaddon said. "It's a different

world now than when you were sent downstairs. Things change."

"Why?" The question left Luce's lips as a growl. "Why is it different *now*?"

"Because of you," Abaddon said. "Losing someone special in your life has a way of changing you. If God's favorite son could fall so far, so hard, then no one was immune. I guess He realized we weren't as infallible as He made us out to be, and if He didn't extend the same courtesy, the same forgiveness, to us, He would lose a lot more than He could bear."

The explanation did nothing to soothe Luce's aggression. It was what he had fought for, what he had lost his Grace over, and he had spent thousands of years trapped in Hell for it, punished for daring to question their Father, and as soon as he was gone, everyone else was given exactly what he wanted. *How is that fair?*

"It's not fair," Abaddon agreed, tapping into Luce's thoughts when his guard dropped, his anger opening his mind. "And it's still not enough, frankly. Yeah, we're free to think as we want, but we're still shackled when it comes to what we do. If I slipped and acted on my impulses, Michael would show up here and annihilate me. How many brothers and sisters have we lost because they fell victim to temptation? Azreal, Dinah, Benjamin, Luna, Maylin, Samuel..."

Luce cut in. "Samuel chose to fall."

"Even worse." Abaddon scoffed. "Look at what happened to his sister."

Luce tensed at the mention of Serah, the bitter sting running deep.

"Sex is forgivable... *expected*... between those that are in love, committed to each other, but what happens when the one you love can't love you back?" Abaddon asked. "How is it fair that she lost her Grace for loving someone incapable of love?"

Those words were like a knife in the chest, severing something inside of Luce. He was up off the stool, grabbing the collar of Abaddon's shirt, and yanking him off the bar in the blink of an eye. Abaddon hit the floor hard, the rush of energy from the impact knocking over the stool, the eyes of people in the bar turning to it, startled. They didn't see the guardian pinned to the floor, didn't see the fallen angel on top of him, pressing the blade of the golden Heavenly knife to his old friend's throat.

Abaddon laid still, eyes wide with surprise.

Luce's stark black wings had sprouted from his back, casting the bar in shadows, as if the lights had dimmed. The electricity flickered and lightening flashed outside, thunder clapping in the distance, as Luce let go of his rage, unleashing the negative energy that had again started building in him.

He usually purged it in the pit, day after day, torturing the inhabitants of Hell. Up here, it had nowhere to go, simmering inside of him, creeping beneath his skin. His nostrils flared, eyes black as the pit, flickering red as he glared at Abaddon, the blade close to slicing the skin.

He could do it. He could plunge the knife in and yank it back out without so much as a morsel of heartache, putting the Guardian out of his misery. His Grace would explode from him, and Luce could feel the tingle on his skin from anticipation. Some of it would seep into his system as he breathed it in, absorbing it, and he craved it, like an addict needing a hit.

Yes, he could do it.

Maybe he would.

Slowly, a smile curved Abaddon's lips as he relaxed back against the floor. "There's the Lucifer I remember... all the passion, none of the pretense."

Luce stared at him for a moment before pulling the knife away from his neck and returning it to safekeeping. He stood up, his wings disappearing, as Abaddon zapped to his feet. The angel smoothed his clothes as he shook his head, leaping right back up on the bar and stretching out.

"You may not admit it out loud, but I can see it in your eyes," Abaddon said. "The idea of having the world for yourself still intrigues you. You want it... want what you were robbed of."

The woman from earlier came over, picking up the knocked-over stool and sitting down on it, not noticing as she brushed up against Luce. She ordered more shots, Abaddon's attention drifting right back to her, his eyes scanning her body like he were studying a work of art.

"And all I'm saying," Abaddon said, "is that as good as looking can be, someday I'd like to have the chance to touch."

"What does that have to do with me?"

Abaddon waited until the woman walked away again to look at Luce. "Everything."

Two

Six months is the blink of an eye when you're eternal.

Hours turned to days turned to weeks turned to months. Luce barely registered the change in time. Winter became Spring, which somehow bloomed Summer. The white coldness that had taken Serah from him was now long gone as everything again turned lively and green.

Luce wandered, and wallowed, occasionally visiting Abaddon out of sheer curiosity of what plan the Guardian was hatching, but he mostly kept to himself.

Still, nobody bothered him.

He found himself continually being drawn to Chorizon, drawn to the woman who didn't even remember he existed. He spent countless hours, days, weeks, watching Serah as she adjusted to life as a mortal. She was his very own living indication that the world continued on. She was alive, breathing, and thinking, visible to everyone, her heart steadily beating.

Once a second.

Sixty beats a minute.

3,600 times an hour.

Over and over, day after day. In the past six months, her heart had beat over sixteen million times. Luce counted sometimes, listening to it even when he couldn't see her, her pulse a constant reminder that she was real.

That it all had been real.

He became attuned to the rhythm, like it was a secret melody produced just for him. He could tell when she was happy, or sad, could tell when she grew excited, or agitated, all from the sound her heart made.

It had become an obsession, a necessity, like her heart beating was the only thing keeping him from disappearing.

Maybe it was pathetic.

Maybe *he* was pathetic.

But Lucifer didn't give a shit how it looked. He couldn't have Serah, but he could hold onto this part of her, and nobody was going to take that away.

Not now, anyway.

Not as long as he could help it.

It was the middle of the afternoon one warm

summer day. Lucifer was strolling down the sidewalk in Chorizon, hands in his pockets, enjoying the breeze that he'd oddly grown appreciative of being able to feel again. He could easily zap where he was going, but what was the point?

No sense rushing when there was nothing else to do.

He strolled past people jogging, kids playing, dogs walking... the animals were the only ones that ever reacted to him. The cats would hiss, and the dogs would bark, and whatever human happened to be nearby would tell them to shut the fuck up because there was nothing there, nobody around, oblivious to the fact that the one they considered the devil, the ultimate evil, was so close he could hear their words.

It amused Lucifer.

He wondered how long this would all last.

Six more months? Six years? Another six thousand? He couldn't fathom it. In even sixty years, the world around him would be vastly different, and the woman he watched would likely cease to exist. The blink of an eye to him; an entire lifetime to her.

He paused outside the community center, hearing her heartbeat across the street.

What would he have when he didn't have this?

This afternoon marked exactly six months... six months since Michael carved the dreaded symbol in Serah's chest in this spot, a damnation Lucifer negated by plunging his knife through it, taking her wings.

He'd been created for that reason—to maintain order, to lead his kind down a path of righteousness, but instead he'd been the one to lead them away. He urged them to follow him, to rebel, being the catalyst for the de-winging he'd been spared from at the end.

He lurked there, watching as Serah stood along the sidewalk, leaning back against the trunk of an old tree. The children at the school were letting out, but Serah scarcely seemed to notice, her attention fixed on the community center near Luce instead.

The pop of static behind Luce was loud. He didn't have to turn his head to know who it was. The strong stench, like stagnant water, hit him so hard he cringed. *Disgusting.* His insides coiled from the sudden tension, anger manifesting that hadn't existed just a moment ago.

Michael.

It took every ounce of strength within Luce to not react. He stared straight ahead, trying to focus on the sound of the heartbeat, as his hand slowly reached toward the golden knife he kept concealed.

"That's unnecessary." Michael's voice was as grating as rough sandpaper as Luce wrapped his hand around the weapon. "I haven't come here to fight."

"Then why have you come?"

"The same reason you're here, I suspect."

Michael stepped forward, pausing beside Luce, a mere foot separating the two. Luce's hand remained on the handle of his blade, prepared to defend himself, but deep down he knew it was unnecessary.

Michael, as misguided as Luce believed him to be, wasn't a liar. There wasn't a devious cell inside of him. If he said he hadn't come to fight, he meant it.

But Luce was still on edge by his presence.

"You shouldn't be here," Luce said, his voice laced with venom.

"Neither should you," Michael responded casually. "But that hasn't stopped you from visiting her every day."

Luce cut his eyes at him. "You've been keeping tabs on me."

"Of course," Michael said. "Do you expect any less?"

No, he didn't. "Business or personal?"

Michael turned to him, their eyes meeting. "Excuse me?"

"Were you ordered to keep tabs on me?" Luce asked. "Because babysitting was never part of an Archangel's job description."

Michael glared at him, the same anger Luce felt reflected in his brother's eyes. "I do it because I must."

Luce shook his head and turned away. That didn't answer his question, but getting any more information from his brother would require torture, and Luce wasn't in the mood for that today. "Well, I haven't convinced anyone to take a bite out of an apple lately, so I think we're all pretty safe for the time being."

"We won't be safe until you're back in the pit where you belong, miscreant."

Luce's lips twisted with amusement. "I've missed you too, brother."

From the corner of his eye, Luce saw Michael flinch at the word 'brother', but he didn't dispute the relationship this time. Michael glared at him for a moment longer before his gaze also shifted across the street.

They both watched in silence as a little girl stopped to speak to Serah, asking her questions about who she was and if she were lost.

"Have you shown yourself to her?" Michael asked after a moment, his voice a low growl.

58

"You tell me," Luce said. "You've been keeping tabs, remember?"

"You must've done it when I wasn't watching," Michael accused. "You showed yourself to her. You're trying to corrupt her!"

"I've done no such thing."

"Then why does she know your face?" Michael asked. "How does she recall your image?"

Luce tensed. "She doesn't."

Before Luce could react, Michael grabbed ahold of him, the sword of fire appearing out of thin air. He threw Luce to the ground, the tip of the sword pressing against his chest, right where his beating heart would be... if he had one of those. "She does! I just saw it!"

Luce didn't give those words any time to sink in as he reacted defensively. He threw Michael off of him, pulling his knife. He was quick, and nearly got him, nearly *stabbed* him, when a sudden warm glow surrounded Michael seconds before he vanished into thin air. A lingering tingle coated Luce's skin as he stood there, suddenly all alone. "Fuck."

Called away in the knick of time.

Lucky bastard.

Luce shoved the knife away, his wings retreating

as he turned back to Serah just as the little girl walked away. Serah's attention once more drifted across the street, this time settling on the space he occupied. Confusion laced her soft features.

Luce was just as confused looking at her.

Could she remember him?

Was that even possible?

Michael stood in the throne room with his head down, his gaze on his bare feet. He breathed heavily, his chest rising and falling from agitation, not from a need of oxygen. Air was nothing to him. He wasn't human.

He never would be.

His dedication and loyalty to his Father was everlasting, but an unfamiliar sensation bubbled inside of him, strangling him, straining him. He was angry... *so very angry.*

"Wrath," a calm voice said.

Michael turned, eyes meeting his Father. He sat in His throne, casually watching Michael, a view of the street projected around them. The atmosphere was calm, as was Satan.

Reignite

"Lucifer," his Father said. "You can call him by his name, son."

Michael stared at Him. He could still feel the anger vibrating through him. Wrath? *Impossible.* Michael wasn't a sinner, but wrath was a sin. How could he be afflicted with it?

"Your brother tends to have that effect on those around him," He said, waving to the seat beside His throne, wordlessly telling Michael to sit down.

For the first time in his existence, the Archangel didn't obey right away. "What's happening to me?"

A soft, understanding smile greeted him. "Sit down, Michael."

Michael didn't hesitate this time, taking the seat. Silently, his attention drifted to the projecting image. Satan stared at Serah longingly, not showing himself, but Michael knew Serah felt the same pull. He'd seen it in her mind, the draw she felt toward the one in all black who consumed her thoughts and visited her dreams. She longed for him, desired him, although she didn't know why, the sort of craving Michael still felt when he looked into her eyes.

Another sensation twisted Michael, vaguely like the anger, but more focused. Concentrated.

"Envy. Dare I say with a dash of lust?"

Seven deadly sins, and his Father was sensing almost half of them emanating from him?

"More than half," He chimed in calmly, reading Michael's thoughts. "Gluttony, for you needlessly want to claim all of her for yourself, and greed, because you don't want to share... and let's not forget pride, because you believe you deserve her so much more than your brother does."

Michael hung his head in shame. Six out of seven? All that was left was sloth.

"Nobody can accuse you of being lazy, son." He reached over and laid a hand on Michael's shoulder, the simple touch sending a wave of calm through him. All at once Michael felt the resentment fade away, a sense of peace settling over him. "You've hardly taken a moment of rest in the past six months."

"How can I rest with him out there?"

"Is it him being out there that worries you? Or is it *her*?"

"What do you mean?"

"I mean are you more afraid of your brother succeeding or of her failing?"

Michael considered that, his gaze fixed to the projecting image. Nothing seemed to matter more to Satan than listening to Serah's heartbeat. It had become an obsession to the fallen angel, something that terrified Michael.

He remembered the last time Satan became obsessed with a beating heart.

It had changed everything.

"I'm afraid those are the same thing, Father," Michael admitted. "I'm afraid he'll corrupt another innocent mortal, and I can't just stand around and do nothing this time."

"It's mesmerizing, isn't it?"

Lucifer sat alone in a section of vast white space in Heaven. Or at least, he *thought* he was alone. But the voice behind him shattered the moment of peaceful silence, pulling him from the depths of his thoughts.

He glanced beside him as his brother sat down. Michael looked on in awe, his gaze fixed straight ahead at their Father's newest creation before them.

Earth.

It was the middle of the third day since the project had begun. An abundance of green was growing on the land, the first stitch of life appearing. Lucifer had been sitting there since it started, watching every

J.M. Darhower

moment with conflicting feelings.

"Yes," he said. "It's certainly something."

"I wonder why He's making it," Michael said. "Do you have any idea?"

They knew what it was from the beginning, but *why* had evaded them. Blessed with knowledge, but so far robbed of insight. Lucifer had been trying to riddle it out on his own since it started. He was the closest to their Father, the only one ever granted time alone with Him, but even he had little more than a guess.

He'd been made to leave the throne room when it all started, as if it were supposed to be a surprise. He had a few theories, the current overwhelming him with thoughts of love.

"I think it's paradise," Lucifer said quietly. "A home for His children."

"Home," Michael repeated. "I like the sound of that."

The first sprinkling of color started to appear, what Lucifer seemed to instinctively know as flowers. Although angels weren't all-knowing, they possessed an innate knowledge thanks to their connection to their Father. Lucifer watched with morbid fascination as the plants bloomed, dotting the landscape.

Beautiful.

His lips slowly turned up into a smile. "Me, too."

Michael sat beside him in silence for a long while, watching the landscape shift as another day dawned. Surrounding the Earth, the sun and the moon formed, stars appearing in the sky, seasons created right before their eyes. It was amazing, full of their Father's love.

A true gift.

Lucifer couldn't wait until it was finished. He looked forward to calling it *home*.

Day four breezed by, dawning day five.

Waves crashed against the land on earth, the water now teeming with life. Lucifer stared in wonder. Thousands upon thousands of different creatures had popped up before his eyes, each one unique and mesmerizing. His Father's ingenuity was beyond anything Lucifer imagined. There were ones with the ability to create, others that could fly; from a massive gentle giant in the ocean to the tiniest speck of a creature in the sky.

Lucifer's chest was so full of love he felt like he would burst if he felt anymore.

The day came and went, the creativity not stopping. Creatures appeared on land, animals of all kind, just as elaborate and breathtaking. He sat in awe, his brother silently by his side, as time wore on and the world began to flourish.

How much more could their Father bless them with?

It was during the sixth day, in a glorious garden, when another creature formed, molded out of the earth. Unlike the four-legged animals, and the ones with scales, and gills, and fins, this creature looked eerily like *him*.

Lucifer watched in shock as the first human came to life.

For the first time in days, his Father's voice could be heard.

Welcome, my child.

The voice was strong and mighty, not spoken out loud, but heard in the mind. Lucifer thought God was speaking to him, one of the few who were blessed enough to hear His voice, when the man on earth responded. "Thank you, Father."

Confusion ran through Lucifer.

He could only gape as the human carried on a conversation with God. Adam was his name, and he was tasked with naming all of the other living creatures, a job he took on happily. Cattle, and cats; Fish, and fowl. The naming went on for most of the day, until they ran out of nameless creatures and

Adam was alone.

Lucifer could hear his Father again then, hear his musing about how His new child needed a companion. Adam went to sleep, and from him spawned a second human, a woman named Eve.

A wife for Adam.

"Be fruitful, and multiply, and replenish the earth, and subdue it," He told them. "And have dominion over the fish of the sea, and over the fowl of the air, and over every living thing that moveth upon the earth."

A sensation Lucifer never encountered before twisted inside of him. He felt as if he were tied in knots, pulled in different directions, like part of him might break. There's no way he really heard what he thought he just heard. He had to have misinterpreted. There had to be a mistake.

There was no way their Father just gave earth to this *human*.

"Home," Michael said. "For His children."

Lucifer glanced at his brother. Michael was smiling, still watching it all with awe. He looked genuinely elated about everything that was happening, while Lucifer felt anything but.

This paradise was supposed to be for them.

Wasn't it?

The afternoon air was warm, the sun shining brightly in the sky, not a single cloud to be seen anywhere. The blue went on for as far as Serah could see, crisp and clear. The color reminded her of a set of eyes that frequented her dreams, a set of eyes that watched when she was awake, haunting her.

They were eyes that held countless secrets, eyes that told a thousand stories, but none of which Serah could understand. They spoke to her, implored her, but she couldn't hear what they had to say. It was a whisper of a memory; he was an apparition, there one second and gone the next, fading into thin air like he were made of dust, and the tiniest breath would blow him away. She wasn't even sure if he actually existed, but he was real to her.

If only she could think of his name.

It hung on the tip of her tongue, swallowed back again and again.

She wondered if she were crazy... if she were legitimately full-blown, call-the-doctors insane. She still knew nothing of the person she had been, nothing of where she'd come from or where she was supposed to be.

The only thing she knew was *him*.

But then again, she didn't even really know him, considering she didn't know his name, or if he were more than a figment of her imagination.

Ugh, maybe I am insane.

Serah walked down the street, heading away from the motel one afternoon, wandering the same familiar neighborhoods she'd wandered every day since the accident. She greeted people warmly as she passed them, her eyes flickering to the windows of the shops as she strolled by, catching sight of the stranger's reflection in the glass with hers, always just a few steps behind.

She knew if she turned around, he wouldn't be there. Nobody would be.

She was strolling along when she came upon the community center, the door propped open to let the air flow in as voices spilled out into the street. Serah stalled in front of the building, surveying it for a moment. She felt a certain draw to the place that she couldn't explain, like she'd been here before.

Curious, she stepped inside. The place was lit up, filled with rows of flimsy metal chairs—maybe three-dozen, but less than half of them were used. Serah slid into the closest one by the door, going undetected. A man standing at the front spoke softly, words washing through Serah. She listened silently, hands folded on her lap.

Something about it all felt familiar to her.

Church.

She fucking went to *church*.

Did she realize she was going there? Luce didn't know. No matter how hard he tried to get a grasp on her, it stayed as foggy as if she were submerged underwater and trying to talk through it.

The human mind always was a mystery to him.

He stood in the middle of the street, in the exact same spot where he'd lost her, and glared at the community center, listening to the voice inside.

...Satan disguises himself as an angel of light...

...The devil sinneth from the beginning...

...Satan hath desired you...

Always the bad, none of the good.

"There is no good."

Lucifer closed his eyes at those words, spoken from the sidewalk behind him. He'd sensed her essence in the area when he followed Serah here, but he'd hoped she was too preoccupied to bother him.

Hannah.

"Lying lips are abomination to the Lord," Lucifer said, an odd tingle of satisfaction deep inside of him. Oh, what irony... he was quoting scripture to rebuke someone who still had Grace.

"I don't lie," Hannah said, stepping out into the street behind him. "There is no good in Satan. He's the enemy, the lying snake, pure evil that needs eradicated. The name alone says so."

"I hear you, sister. Heard you last time, too. You're just wasting your fucking breath at this point."

He cut his eyes to the right when she paused beside him. Her gaze was trained on him, eyes narrowed suspiciously. He sensed no fear from her, and her anger was still present, but it wasn't as strong as before. No, it had given way to something tougher—grief. It was easy to be pissed, to throw blame, but it was a completely different game trying to come to terms with heartache.

Angels aren't meant to mourn their own kind.

"Why are you here, Hannah?" he asked skeptically. "Your kind doesn't think twice after we fall. You write us off like we never existed."

"We do," she agreed. "But something happened."

"What happened?"

She didn't answer that, but Lucifer saw it all in her mind as she purposely dropped her guard for him. It all played out, every moment of the short-lived apocalypse, every gritty detail Hannah had witnessed. And he saw the last memory like a movie, Hannah helping Serah escape the woods in Hellum Township.

"I'm nothing," Serah said. "I succumbed to the snake's temptation. I unleashed Satan."

"You were enchanted by Lucifer. He was an Archangel, Ser, the most glorious one ever created. I can't fault you for falling for him."

"I am," she whispered. "Literally."

A rush of black shadows whipped past, blanketing the land as far as the eyes could see. Serah gasped, struggling for air.

"Michael released the reapers," Hannah said. "It's only a matter of time before they track him down."

"Then what?" Serah asked.

"You know the prophecy—Satan will be destroyed once and for all."

Lucifer turned away from her. He didn't need—or want—to see anymore. But he grasped Hannah's issue, knew exactly what had changed everything: he was still here. "The prophecy didn't come true."

"Or it did," she said. "Either the prophecy was wrong, or you're not Satan."

"Which one is it?"

"I haven't decided," she admitted. "Serah believed you weren't him enough to fall for you."

Lucifer shook his head. "If I weren't him, she wouldn't have fallen."

As soon as he said it, it dawned on him that this conversation was the complete opposite of the last time he spoke to Hannah, where she'd called him Satan and he rejected the notion. Now she was conceding that maybe he wasn't evil after all, and he was still trying to prove her wrong.

Clearly, there was no winning.

Luce stared at the door of the community center in silence for a moment, listening as the preacher talked about resisting temptation. His thoughts drifted, his eyes on Serah sitting right inside the door, until a loud crack echoed through the street and a big gray mass abruptly blocked his view.

A Dominion.

"You've got to be fucking kidding me," he muttered, stepping to the side to see around the monotone angel. Those drab winged fuckers always annoyed him.

"Is, uh... is there a new task?" Hannah asked, nervousness straining her voice. Being caught anywhere with Luce clearly hadn't been a part of Hannah's plans.

"Yes," the Dominion said.

"What is it?" she asked. "What do I need to do?"

"Nothing," the Dominion said. "The task isn't for you, Virtue."

Lucifer cut his eyes at the Dominion, seeing he was staring at him. "You're kidding, right?"

"The Dominion do not joke."

"No shit." They'd been created without a sense of humor. All work and no play does a boring ass angel make. "But you must be mistaken, because I'm not one of your drones that you can order around. You don't get to tell me what to do, not then, and certainly not now."

The Dominion glared at him. Lucifer heard the bitterness in his mind, words he'd never verbalize. *The arrogance of Archangels is astounding, but the fallen miscreant takes it to another level.*

Lucifer smirked at that, amused, and shook his head as he turned away from the angel. "Run along and tell Daddy I'm not interested in whatever worthless assignment He's trying to shove on me."

74

That clearly wasn't the answer the Dominion wanted, but instead of pressing the matter, the angel nodded in acknowledgment and apparated away.

"The Dominion's tasks aren't negotiable," Hannah said. "It's God's will."

"So?" Lucifer said. "It's been His will for me to be in Hell for six thousand years, but that didn't stop me from finding a way to escape."

A way that stole Hannah's friend from her as a consequence. Lucifer heard those words, spoken silently. He stared straight ahead as church services came to an end, the few parishioners filtering out. Serah lingered in her seat for a moment before getting up and walking out, strolling down the street without ever actually participating.

Lucifer stared at her until she disappeared from sight. He could still hear her heartbeat after that, pounding steadily.

He said nothing to Hannah, no goodbye, no words of well-wishing. They weren't friends. One thing connected them, and that thing knew nothing of either of them anymore. He strolled to the community center and stepped inside, his footsteps methodic.

What do you know? I didn't catch on fire.

The preacher still stood at the front, absently

flipping through his worn bible, taking notes.

Lucifer paused right in front of him, their faces mere inches apart. He was skimming through Genesis, his next sermon to focus on the beginning of time, the rise of man and the fall of Satan.

It would be easy, so very easy, to just flip the switch and become visible, literally terrifying the life from the man. But what was the point? Another human dead, gone from the world, but there were seven billion more just like him out there.

Last time Lucifer stood on Earth, there were only *two*.

Thump.

Thump.

Thump.

Over and over.

Again and again.

It was Lucifer's first time on Earth. He stood deep in the Garden of Eden, shielded from weak human eyes, surveying the one called Adam.

For creatures that looked much like him on the surface, Adam seemed inherently inferior. He wasn't even advanced enough to sense an angel in front of him. Why did he deserve such a gift like paradise?

The thumping came from Adam's chest, strong and steady. Most other living creatures on earth had the same rhythmic sound echoing from them, but Adam's was louder. It was his life force. Where Lucifer was filled with Grace, the warm glow of radiant energy, burning as bright as the stars now viewed above, Adam was filled with something else.

Blood.

Lucifer had seen it, had watched as the man accidentally pricked his finger on a thorn and spilled a drop of red onto the earth. It caused the man pain, something as harmless as a beautiful bush of roses injuring him.

How fragile.

How weak.

The thumping in his chest had grown louder, harder, more frenzied when it happened, like something in his chest was tied to the pain.

"It's called a heart."

Lucifer turned away from Adam at the sound of his Father's voice, finding Him there in the garden. He'd heard his thoughts. He'd been watching.

"The sound you hear is his heart beating," He

continued, stepping closer. "Its what keeps Adam alive."

"How long will he live?"

"Forever."

Forever.

Inferior yet blessed with the same eternal life as Lucifer.

"I wouldn't call humans inferior," He said. "Just different. They have weaknesses you don't possess, but they also have gifts. They can't sense you, but they can sense things that you can't."

"Like what?"

His Father motioned toward the rose bush, the same one that Adam had injured himself with. "Smell this."

"What?"

"Place your nose to the flower."

Lucifer did as he was told, but nothing happened.

"You can't smell it," He explained. "Everything around you has a fragrance. You can see these things—these flowers, these trees—but Adam experiences them. He breathes them in, he tastes them, *lives* them. He's one with Earth; you're one with Heaven. You're different creatures, Lucifer."

Lucifer turned back to Adam, observing him as he

interacted with Eve. Both were filled to the brim with love—love for each other, love for their Father. "What's their purpose?"

"To exist, and to love, and to worship," He said. "They're my children."

Lucifer hesitated. "And what's my purpose?"

"You know yours."

To see their Father's will through, to serve Him, and obey Him. "Does that will include these humans? Does serving you mean serving... *them*?"

Lucifer didn't have to wait for Him to respond. He knew the truth. But it still nearly knocked him over when the answer resounded around him. "Yes."

Lucifer stared at the humans. Just moments ago he'd viewed them as inferior, but now he felt differently. If anything, it was clear to him now that *he* was the subordinate here.

"That's not it at all, my son," He interjected.

"Son," Lucifer said quietly. "Am I your son?"

"Of course you are."

"It doesn't seem that way." He shook his head, turning away from Adam to glance at his Father. "Not anymore."

Serah's heart was racing fast, battering her ribcage like a jackhammer. Luce heard it the moment he apparated in the parking lot outside the motel. It was coming from a room on the far end of the second floor. He tensed, straining his senses, trying to make sense of her excitement, but it was a puzzle that wouldn't come together without seeing the picture.

He had to see.

He had to know.

In a flash, he zapped straight up, appearing just inside the open door of the dingy motel room. He sensed no one else, spotting Serah right away, the tension in his muscles receding as confusion washed through him.

She was *dancing*.

He could faintly detect the music from this distance, streaming straight to her from the tiny speakers lodged in her ears. She danced to the beat of the song, swaying and bouncing, oblivious to everything around her as she absently changed the sheets on a bed.

Luce could do nothing but stare. Common sense told him to back away, to put some distance between them before he did something stupid, but it was hard to be logical when you're a passion-fueled creature not known for doing the right thing.

Ever.

He hadn't been this close to her since she woke up a new person... a mortal. He could smell her, the natural sweetness, and the light fragrance of flowers, with a hint of sweat lingering on her skin. And he could feel her warmth from where he stood, feel it radiating from her and absorbing into him. Her heartbeat was louder so close, tempting him, calling to him.

What harm would it do to touch her one time? Just once, a graze of her skin, to stand flush against her body and breathe her in. She'd never know, as long as he was willing to let go.

In a moment of weakness, he took a step toward her, just as she swung in his direction. Her gaze flickered up toward the door as she abruptly stopped dancing, eyes going wide. Her heart stalled, the brief moment of silence screaming loudly to Lucifer, ripping him to shreds from the inside out. His worst fear was coming to life, even for a second: Serah's heart wasn't beating.

He felt the pain gripping his own chest.

But then her heart kicked into overdrive, pounding violently as she startled, yanking the music from her ears. A gasp resounded through the room when her lips parted. She stared through him, around him, at something near him, but there was no way she stared at him.

No way.

It just wasn't possible. They may have stood in the same room, but they were on entirely different planes. A human couldn't see an angel unless they purposely showed themselves, and he'd never shown himself to a human. *Never.*

"It's you," she whispered.

Lucifer stared at her with disbelief. *Me?*

"I, uh... I'm sorry," she said quickly. "I didn't know anyone was in here... I didn't think... I mean, I thought... well, check out was an hour ago, and all your things were gone, and I didn't realize..."

She stammered on and on. Lucifer was dumbfounded, remaining quiet and gaping at her like he was the one seeing a ghost.

"I can go, and come back," she continued. "I mean, if you still need the room, that is. I don't want to be in the way."

She started for the door, trying to go around him. On a whim, Lucifer stepped in her path, still expecting her to go right through him, like humans always did, but her footsteps stalled. Her heart skipped another beat as she swallowed thickly. He could sense it then, something angels were trained to detect, the one thing that surrounded him day in and day out down in the pit. *Fear.*

"Can you see me?" he asked, arching an eyebrow in question.

She stared at him blankly for a moment, and he still thought maybe she stared through him, until she slowly nodded her head. "Of course."

"You see me," he said again. "You know me?"

"Yes," she said tentatively, her heartbeat so frantic it was like a bass drum. Hope swelled through Luce. She really remembered him. "Well, no... I don't know you. I've seen you, but I don't know who you are."

His stomach dropped. "You don't?"

"Uh, no... should I?"

"But you can see me," he said for the third time, raising his voice. He ignored her question, the voice deep inside of him screaming 'how the fuck could you ever forget?' "You've seen me before."

"Yes, of course," she said, her voice quaking as she took a step back, wrapping her arms around her chest. "What's wrong with you?"

He was scaring her. Closing his eyes, he tried to

calm himself down, but it was senseless. There was no way this was happening. It was a dream, or a fucking nightmare, punishment from his Father. He hadn't escaped the pit at all... maybe this was his new Hell, forever to be teased and taunted by her existence, close but still so far away.

Turning around, he stepped out of the open doorway and glanced around, freezing when he saw someone walking down the tier toward him. He stepped toward them as they approached the room next door to unlock it. Lucifer waved his hand in the woman's face, but she didn't react, brushing against him without noticing him there.

Once she was gone, he looked around again, seeing Serah watching him incredulously from the other room. He stood on the tier, looking around the neighborhood, seeing people walking by on the street below, others lingering in the parking lot.

He shouted, trying to get their attention, but his voice was lost to them, the wrong frequency for mortal ears.

Serah flinched, though, covering her ears and cringing when he turned in her direction. He stalked toward her, pointing at her, as she retreated back into the room.

"What's wrong with you?" he growled, echoing her question. It clearly wasn't him that was fucked up—it was her. Mortals couldn't see him, couldn't hear him, couldn't sense him, but she was holding a conversation with him as if this shit were normal. "How can you see me?"

"You're crazy," she said, something akin to terror flashing across her face. "Oh God, maybe I'm crazy. I'm really crazy, aren't I?" She plopped down on the edge of the bed, long ago forgetting she was in the middle of making it. She cradled her head in her hands. "I've lost my mind. You're not real. You're not really here."

Lucifer wanted to console her, to clear this all up and make sense of the mess, but he was speechless. How was this happening? He opened his mouth and closed it again.

What could he say?

"You're not crazy."

She laughed loudly with disbelief. "Then what am I?"

"You're—"

Before he could get out his sentence, a strong tingle shot down his spine, a brilliant glow surrounding him. The light exploded to a ball of bright white, blinding him for a second, before the world around him cleared.

"—an angel."

He finished his declaration quietly, the words senseless. He was so far away she would never hear. His feet were planted somewhere he hadn't been in thousands of years, a place he never expected to see under these circumstances... a room he didn't anticipate an invitation to anytime soon.

Or ever again.

Heaven.

It was exactly how he recalled it. Lucifer stood in front of the throne, eyes meeting his Father's for the first time since his fall. Beside Him sat Michael, in the seat that had been created for Lucifer. Anger simmered inside of him, every inch of him coiling and tightening, so tense he couldn't move. Literally.

His gaze drifted to his feet. Sigils were burned into the floor around him, the same markings that had not long ago tarnished his skin, trapping him in Hell. He laughed dryly under his breath. Un-fucking-believable. Imprisoned in Heaven.

Invited, but clearly not trusted. He was confined in a box of enchanted space, barred from stepping outside of it, of hurting anyone away from it.

Luce's eyes returned to the throne. He cocked an

eyebrow in question, but he said nothing.

His Father stared back, calm, collected. His nonchalant demeanor only fueled Luce's rage. How dare He bring him here and confine him like a rabid animal needing caged. He was done being restrained.

"Do you have nothing to say, son?"

"Fuck you."

He spat the curse with everything in him, but it still wasn't enough for a reaction from Him. Michael, on the other hand, flinched.

"He that blasphemes the name of the Lord shall be put to death," Michael declared.

Luce turned to him. "Well, fuck you, too."

His Father slowly shook His head, with just one look making Luce feel like that same disgruntled disappointment he'd been back in the Garden of Eden. "You still hold onto so much anger."

"Can you blame me?"

Rhetorical question, but He answered anyway. "Yes."

"Good. Great. Glad we could have this talk. Now put me back where you got me from."

"Trust in The Lord with all your heart," Michael said, "and do not lean on your own understanding."

Luce needlessly blinked a few times and regarded his brother as he recited scripture. He'd had the good book quoted to him more times than he cared to count since he escaped the pit, like those words were supposed to mean something to him. He was getting tired of hearing it.

"Not a fan of literature?" He asked, hearing Luce's thoughts. Of course. He heard all, knew all, saw all... Luce was sure Michael could whip out a dozen scriptures stating just that.

"I'm more of a Stephen King fan."

"So you prefer fiction to reality?"

Luce shrugged a shoulder. "Reality is subjective. Down in the pit, it's all real."

Michael started to throw out yet another nugget of biblical wisdom, but their Father raised a hand to silence him.

"That's not what I wanted for you, son."

"But it's what you gave me," he replied. "So if you don't mind, I'd appreciate it if you'd put me back where you found me."

"I will happily return you to the lake of fire," Michael interjected. "It would be my pleasure."

"Your pleasure?" Luce asked, cocking an eyebrow at him.

Michael nodded in confirmation. "Nothing would please me more."

"Nothing?" Luce laughed mockingly. "I tell you, Mikey, if that's how you get your thrills these days, I suggest finding another angel to get your rocks off with. You know, since you got the last one de-winged."

Michael was up out of his seat, hastily approaching in the blink of an eye. He stopped right in front of Luce, mere inches of space between the two. Luce stood as still as a statue, just waiting for Michael to move a bit closer... just waiting for him to cross the sigils so he could get his hands on him.

"You did it to her," Michael growled. "You destroyed her."

"I'm not the one who tried to cast her into Hell."

"But it's your fault it happened!"

"Enough." Their Father's voice rang through the room, not raised at all, but it held all the force of a ferocious scream. "You two sound like bickering children... dare I say, like brothers."

Michael didn't seem to like that assessment and tried to speak up. "But—"

"I said that's enough," He said, waving beside the throne. "Take your seat, Michael."

Hesitantly, Michael retreated, sitting back down. Luce glared at him, his Father's words rubbing him the wrong way. *Take your seat, Michael.* That seat had been created for him, not Michael.

"It was," He said, once again hearing his thoughts. "But you forfeited it, giving up your place in Heaven."

"So why am I here then?" Luce asked. "Scold me, smite me, do whatever you want to do to me, but I'm done with this conversation, so get on with it or let me go."

His Father stared at him, contemplating. When He finally spoke, His words were quiet. "You may mean no harm to her, son, but you know what they say about good intentions."

In an instant, Lucifer was zapped away in another ball of bright white light, reappearing exactly where he had been standing in the motel room. As the room cleared around him, everything coming into focus, His final words ran through Lucifer's mind.

The road to Hell is paved with good intentions.

In this case, probably literally.

"I'm what?"

Lucifer's gaze darted to the bed, to where Serah still sat, staring at him. It felt like he'd been away for half an hour, but he knew it would only be a fraction of a second to her. She would've never noticed he was gone, would've never seen him leave and come back.

She stared at him, waiting for him to finish what he'd been saying before he'd been interrupted.

You're an angel.

Yeah, because that would go over well. She'd either be certain then, that he was crazy, or he'd look like nothing more than a pervert with a cheesy pick-up line. *Did it hurt when you fell from Heaven?*

Of course it did, asshole. I bled out in the fucking street.

He shook his head, brushing it off, as he slowly stepped toward her. She didn't cower away from him, more curious than fearful. Wide-eyed, she stared up at him when he paused in front of her.

"You're dreaming," he said quietly. "I'm nothing more than a figment of your imagination."

Reaching out, he pressed a single fingertip to her forehead, feeling the energy pulsing beneath her skin. It only lasted a second, a mere second of touching her again, before she fell back on the bed.

She was out like a light, fast asleep. She'd wake up after he was gone, and this whole encounter would be nothing but a vague dream.

Sighing, he gazed at her for a moment before leaving. He fucking hated when those holy rollers were right.

The humans had it all.

They lavished on earth, innocent and righteous, granted eternal life in paradise. Adam and Eve loved each other, their love sanctified by God, and they showed each other affectionately. They were obedient creatures, as obedient as Lucifer had always been, except they had something he didn't.

Free will.

It was a novel concept he couldn't quite wrap his mind around. The angels were created for a specific reason, to perform tasks dished out by the Dominion, orders from their Father. It was undeniable, unarguable. He spoke and they listened.

But humans were created and set free. Their job was merely to exist, with hope they'd always love God for their gift.

It caused something to twist inside of Lucifer, a shift in his make up, foreign thoughts and feelings invading the Archangel's world. He was a jealous sibling, wondering why his Father loved a different child more than him.

He resented Adam.

The human had everything.

Lucifer stood in the middle of the garden, beneath the Tree of Knowledge, the one and only thing forbidden to these humans. Lucifer lived an existence of obedience, yet these beating-heart creatures' only rule was 'don't touch this tree.'

A tree.

Reaching out, Lucifer ran his fingertips along the smooth bark. It was nothing special, nothing any different than the other trees in the garden. Had God not singled it out as special, none of them would've noticed it. It was a test, Lucifer knew… it was their Father's way of gauging their obedience, how faultless and perfect his beloved humans were.

Bullshit.

The woman named Eve lingered nearby, oblivious to his presence. She cast looks at the tree but never ventured too close. Maybe it was out of love, like their Father believed, but Lucifer detected something else. It was the first time he'd ever felt it. Fear. Fear of what would happen if she touched it, fear of whatever secrets the fruit held. Lucifer watched her for a while, his frustration mounting each second that ticked by.

He leaned back against the tree, crossing his arms over his chest. A green serpent slithered along the branch above him, drawing Eve's attention.

Eat from the tree, he thought, projecting the sentiment directly at her. She tensed as if his silent words rang loud and clear through the garden. Her eyes shifted around, her fear growing, before her gaze turned right back to the serpent.

She thought the creature was speaking to her.

Try the fruit, he thought. *It's the best there is.*

Eve stepped his way, edging closer to the tree than she ever ventured before. Her heartbeat was wild, the thumping like an echo in Lucifer's ears.

Her voice was quiet, her eyes hesitantly on the snake. "We're not supposed to eat from that tree. God told Adam—"

Nonsense, Lucifer thought, cutting her off. *It's the Tree of Knowledge. Don't you think having wisdom is a good thing? Don't you want to be knowledgeable? Don't you want to be closer to Him?*

"But—"

Try it, he thought again. *Touch it. Taste it. Eat the fruit.*

She hesitated, staring long and hard at the tree, before stepping even closer, her body unwittingly flush against Lucifer. Reaching up, she plucked an apple from the branch near the snake and brought it to her lips, hesitating once again, before taking her first bite.

A soft moan escaped the woman's lips as she closed her eyes, juice from the apple running down her chin. A smile curved Lucifer's lips as he watched her savor the forbidden fruit.

He wondered what it tasted like.

The Tree of Knowledge. He wasn't sure what the human got out of it, but he certainly learned something.

His Father's new children weren't as perfect as He hoped.

There's only one thing worse than Hell.

Hell without a King.

The moment Lucifer stepped through the sixth gate, the whirlwind sucking him down to the pit, chaos greeted him. The blur of surroundings around him cleared, the seventh gate in tact. It was different now, the magical translucent shield stronger, the sigils that had once marked Lucifer's skin now burned straight into the gate. It was the only way to keep the demons inside, to keep the evil from crossing through and heading right back onto Earth in Lucifer's absence.

J.M. Darhower

He paused a few feet away, staring at the madness. He wasn't around to keep up the façade—to tidy up, so-to-speak—so it was little more than a bottomless pit of anarchy. Fire raged as demons ran loose, fighting and fucking, torturing and taunting. Every Hell that had existed converged into one gigantic mindfuck of a nightmare.

It turned his stomach.

They were savages.

Luce slowly approached, the gate within reach of his fingertips. Anything inside was trapped there, the reapers constantly attacking anyone who got too close, ripping them to pieces like they'd done to Luce so many times before. He watched it for a moment on the protected side of the gate, contemplating, hesitating, before letting out a deep sigh and stepping right through.

The second he entered Hell, the scenery change. It was like a flood rushing through, wiping away the madness and dousing the fires, the molten lava hardening, the Hell reforming that Serah had seen day in and day out when she approached the gate.

Lucifer's Hell.

Desolation.

Lightning flashed, thunder cracking, rumbling the

ground, knocking demons off their feet. Lucifer's wings had emerged, overshadowing everything, obscuring Hell in a shadowy darkness. Demons immediately stopped what they were doing and bowed down as he stood there, eyes sweeping along them all, anger simmering inside of him.

He said nothing.

With the snap of a finger, they vanished. Back to their cages, forced back into their torment, as Lucifer locked them all away.

All except for one, that is.

Lire.

The demon was not far in front of him, bowed obediently. Lucifer strolled forward, kicking his side hard. "Get up."

Lire scrambled to get to his feet. "My Lord."

"Make sure they're all locked up again," Lucifer said. "You find any stragglers, you let me know and I'll make them regret disobeying me."

"Yes, anything you need." Lire turned to scamper away but paused after a few steps. "My Lord, it's great to see you, but I thought things were well on earth. We were informed you were roaming free."

"I was."

Lire stared at him. "So why are you here?"

Luce had no answer for that. With another snap of the finger, Lire disappeared, vanquished from sight. Why was he here? He didn't know. This is the last place he wanted to be. But being on Earth, being near Serah, not being able to touch her, or be with her?

Well, maybe there were *two* things worse than Hell.

Luce strode right down the long winding dirt path, leading straight to the decrepit castle, passing not another soul along the way. He went inside, went straight to the conference room, retaking his seat on the carved marble throne in front of the long table. Slouching down, he let out an exasperated sigh and pulled the old deck of cards from his pocket.

He didn't play War today.

Today, he played Solitaire.

The plastic bags dug into Serah's skin, cutting off the circulation as she tried to juggle nearly a dozen of them, clutched tightly in her hands and around her wrists.

Getting groceries was a pain. *Literally.*

She strode through the parking lot toward the motel, trying to endure it, but it got to be too much. Groaning, she set down the bags in the middle of the lot and flexed her fingers, bright red from the strain.

She needed a car.

She could afford one with all the money she'd saved working and living at the motel. In fact, she'd made enough the past few months to afford to move out into her own place. Living and working in the same place had gotten to her, messed with her head, so much so she'd passed out on one of the beds last week, fell asleep in the middle of her job.

It wasn't like her at all.

She'd dreamed about the man again, the man who was always around yet wasn't really there at all. It was peculiar, and she could remember him so vividly, every detail of his face, even the sound of his voice. It was the first time in all the times she saw him that he actually spoke to her.

Her boss had offered her a new job, a promotion of sorts, working regular hours at the front desk at night, so Serah figured it was time to move on, settle into a normal routine, try to build a life.

She hadn't seen the stranger since making that decision.

Not that any of it was real, anyway. Not that *he* was real. Her imagination was running wild, conjuring up phantom people in her dreams.

Or maybe you're really crazy, like the doctors suspected. Who has an entire lifetime of memories wiped away in a freak lightning storm?

Sighing, Serah reached down to pick up the bags again when a voice cut through the lot nearby, calling out to her. "Here, let me help you."

She quickly looked up at the sound of the foreign voice with a twinge of an accent, seeing a man she'd never seen before in front of her. A blue suit clung to his frame, his hair long and pulled back. He was unusual looking, his features sharp as chiseled stone right down to the pointy nose. He smiled kindly, though, a tingly sensation creeping along her spine when she looked into his eyes. Bright, bright blue... unnaturally blue... the sort of blue that felt familiar, like a crisp lake full of the coolest, purest water.

It momentarily entranced her. The man wasn't particularly attractive, but those eyes were.

"Uh, okay," she said, blinking away her stupor as

she shivered from the chill. She returned his smile as he easily picked up all of the bags for her. "Thanks."

He nodded. "Sure thing, m'lady. Lead the way." She continued through the parking lot, straight to her room, and unlocked the door. The man set the bags right inside, pausing near the doorway, being nice enough to not enter without her permission.

"I appreciate it," she said again. "Truly."

"Don't mention it," he said. "It's what any gentleman would do."

In the past six months, Serah hadn't encountered many gentlemen. She'd been hit on, catcalled, and even picked on, but not many have gone out of their way to hold open doors or carry things for her.

It was certainly a nice change of pace.

"I'm Sarah," she said politely, holding her hand out to him. "Or, well, you can call me Sarah. That's what everyone calls me now."

He eyed her peculiarly for a moment before reaching out and taking her hand, bringing it up to his mouth, pressing a light kiss to the back of it that made Serah's cheeks flush.

"Sarah," he said. "You can call me Don."

"My Lord!"

The double doors to the conference room flung open unexpectedly, Lire rushing in without knocking. Luce looked up from his cards, eyes narrowed angrily at the interruption. Lire knew better than to just burst in without permission. Luce had been gone six months, sure, but that was nothing compared to the six thousand years he spent down here before that. *How soon they forget.*

Luce was up out of his seat and right in front of Lire before the demon could utter another word. Grasping him around the neck, Luce lifted him off the ground, choking him as he slammed the demon back against the wall beside the door. He flailed, grasping Luce's hand as he struggled against his hold. "I don't recall telling you to enter."

"My Lord," Lire said again, his voice strained. "There's an angel at the gate."

Luce glared at him for a moment, straining his senses to try to feel the heavenly presence, but the gate was much too strong. He could only barely feel anything beyond it. Michael had outdone himself this time. There was no escaping that magic. "What angel?"

"A Dominion," Lire said.

Ah. Luce let go of Lire. The demon dropped to the ground hard as Luce turned around and walked right back over to his marble throne, sitting down in it. He brusquely waved his hand, motioning for Lire to leave when the demon climbed to his feet. "Send them away."

Lire raised his eyebrows with surprise. "You don't wish to speak to them?"

Luce shook his head. In the past he got a kick out of his angelic visitors, entertaining himself by taunting them, teasing them, tempting them... but there was no point anymore. He could convince a hundred of his brothers and sisters to fall, but it wouldn't make a difference. It wouldn't change a fucking thing.

Besides, the Dominion bored him shitless.

Lire scurried out, leaving Luce alone again. He went right back to playing Solitaire.

Every day, like clockwork, the Dominion showed up at the gate. And every day, minutes later, Lire would send him away. It went on for a week—a long, tedious week where Luce barely moved from his chair. Nothing appealed to him anymore.

It was the seventh day, and Luce haphazardly flipped cards around on the table when the doors to the room flung open again. Luce closed his eyes, sighing exasperatedly, as Lire burst in.

"My Lord," he shouted. "The angel—"

"I swear, Lire, if you come to me about that Dominion one more time I will gut you every day for the rest of your miserable existence."

"Not the Dominion," Lire said, his voice bordering on frantic. "It's—"

Before Lire could finish, Luce felt the tingle flow through him, the powerful Grace, so damn familiar, so damn appealing, if it weren't for the pungent odor that accompanied it. "Michael."

Within seconds, the scent of stagnant water filled the air as Lire choked on his words. Luce opened his eyes again, looking toward the doorway to find the demon impaled on the end of Michael's sword. Michael yanked it out, the demon exploding into a blast of smoke and fire, all trace of him vanishing from the room.

Shaking his head, Luce turned back to his cards, shuffling the ones in his hand. "That was pointless. He'll just regenerate by tomorrow in the pit."

"Pointless, maybe," Michael said, "but still satisfying."

"Self-indulgence," Lucifer said. "Isn't there

something in the good book that warns against that?"

"It's not self-indulgence when it's for the greater good," Michael said. "He was evil."

"But he wasn't hurting you," Luce pointed out. "In fact, he was announcing your arrival. You should've thanked him. He seems to think you're a big deal, brother. He probably would've thrown you a parade had you asked."

Michael scoffed. Luce went back to flipping over cards, wordlessly playing his game. After a moment, Michael stepped further into the room. "Nice place you have here."

Luce stopped what he was doing and glanced at Michael, sensing the sarcasm in his voice. So out of character for the hard-ass Archangel. "Why are you here, Michael? Don't get me wrong—it's bold. Before today, Serah was the only one with the guts to step down here, and she only did it because she was desperate for something. So I can't help but wonder what you want from me."

Michael looked at him, his expression stoic. "The Dominion has been summoning you for a week, but you haven't responded."

"Yeah, well, I haven't been in the mood for company."

"You have a task," Michael said, ignoring his mocking remark.

"Look, I'm back where you've wanted me... what more do you expect? Me to throw a fucking housewarming party to prove I'm settling in?"

"A different task," Michael clarified. "An important one."

"Important enough for my little brother to venture into the unhappiest place on Earth to deliver the message?" Luce leaned back in his seat, kicking his feet up as he regarded Michael curiously. He motioned toward the chair at the other end of the table. "Have a seat."

Michael didn't sit. "There is an uprising amongst the angels. Some of your old followers, ones who were once forgiven for their debauchery, are planning another revolt."

"Debauchery," Luce echoed. "That's what we're calling it?"

"What would you call it?"

"I'd call it differing opinions... having reservations."

Michael stared at him. "It doesn't matter what we call it. They are planning to finish what you started."

"Well, good for them," Luce said. "Maybe they'll

have better luck than I did."

"Do you not see the implications of this? What can happen if they're successful? The world will be destroyed, overrun with sin, the humans corrupted beyond saving."

"So?"

"So?" Michael stepped even closer, his voice edging on anger. "You cursed them to the fate of mortality, and you say 'so'? You damned angels to fall to Earth, and then you don't care that the Earth could be destroyed? We watched its creation together! How can you not care? How can you not care when she's there?"

The mention of Serah, even without uttering her name, caused every inch of Luce to tense up. His eyes narrowed as he glared at his brother. "You have a lot of nerve talking to me about her."

"Me?" Michael asked incredulously. "What about what *you* did to her?"

"I gave her a second chance!" Luce said. "When she dies, she'll go back to Heaven, back where she belongs. You tried to damn her to Hell, the one place she should've never been. So who's the evil one here, brother? Who's the one who doesn't care?"

"I was doing my job."

"And that's all it has ever been to you," Luce said. "Work, work, work... but I want to live. I *wanted* to live."

Michael glared at him for a moment before looking around the room. "Nice life you have here."

"Fuck you."

"While you sit here in your self-imposed exile, I'll be off cleaning up your messes yet again," Michael said. "I knew you were corrupted, miscreant, but I never realized what a coward you could be."

"Get out," Luce growled.

"I don't take orders from you," Michael said, standing firmly in spot, defiantly staring at him.

Angrily, Luce slammed his fist down on the long table, the force making the ground rumble as the marble gave way, a jagged lightning bolt shaped fracture running right down the center of it. "Get out!"

His voice echoed through the room as thunder cracked above them, the scenery shifting as his anger broke through. Flames incinerated the floor, surrounding the both of them. Lucifer could feel the intense heat, could smell everything around them singeing, but he knew Michael sensed neither. Michael felt nothing. He smelled nothing.

As far as Lucifer concerned, he was nothing.

Hesitantly, Michael took a step back, nodding. Michael may not fear him, and wouldn't usually stand down, but Luce had the upper hand down here. All it would take was a snap of his finger and Michael would be locked in a cage somewhere, living his worst nightmare.

Luce was tempted. He wondered what that was.

Probably disappointing God.

Turning, Michael started for the exit as the fire wound down, the flames fading back into a floor. He paused when he reached the door but didn't look back. "Abaddon has been showing himself to the humans."

"Doesn't surprise me a bit," Luce muttered. It wasn't a rule, so to speak, but it was certainly frowned upon to purposely be seen without a damn good reason. "Still don't see what it has to do with me."

"He showed himself to *her*," Michael said. "Out of all the humans in the world, why do you think that is?"

"You're lying."

Abaddon wouldn't do that... not with her. Not knowing who she was, not knowing what he knew about Luce.

"I don't lie," Michael said. "You know that."

He did know that. If Michael said it, Michael

thought it was true. He wasn't always right... fuck, he was often wrong... but he believed it.

Michael walked out without another word, leaving Luce alone. He turned his attention back to his cards, shoving against the table and sending them flying through the room, whipping through the air like a tornado.

Luce remembered a time long ago when he'd charmed a naïve human into doing his bidding, tainting her without her knowledge, using her as a pawn in his game.

Seems his old friend was taking a page from his book.

Lucifer stood at the gate, a mere foot from the magical charms locking everyone inside. He could feel the energy pulsating from it, pressing upon his skin, trying to force him further away. Above, the reapers swarmed, sensing his presence, watching and waiting to see what he would do.

Sighing, he pulled the heavenly knife out and eyed it. *I sincerely hope this doesn't backfire.* He wasn't in the mood to be annihilated today. Sure, he'd regenerate, be no worse for wear come tomorrow, or the next day if they completely obliterated him, but it hurt like a son of a bitch being ripped apart, piece-by-piece.

Pulling off his black shirt, he draped it over his shoulder as he brought the knife up to where his heart should be. He winced as the blade cut into his skin, blood oozing to the surface, drops running down his bare chest, coating it with streaks of red. Light radiated from the wound when he cut deep, the pain nearly unbearable. He grit his teeth as he carved the elaborate sigil onto his chest.

The mark of Lucifer.

He hadn't seen it—hadn't *used* it—in a long time, not since it had been traded in for the mark of Satan instead. Each of the Archangels had their own. He just hoped enough of that angel still existed inside of him for it to work. The mark pulsated, the light dim, but it didn't fade from his skin.

Clutching the knife tightly, Lucifer stepped straight into the gate. It resisted, the pain from the mark radiating through his body like a jolt of electricity, frying his insides, but the charms gave way, pushing him through to the other side. It shoved him so hard he lost his balance, nearly falling, as he breathed a deep sigh of relief.

The reapers barely took notice of him once he was outside.

Luce didn't look back, striding away, venturing through the gates and stepping back on Earth. He went straight to Chorizon, straight to the small motel on the outskirts of town. As soon as he arrived, he sensed her there, but she wasn't the only one.

Abaddon.

"Son of a bitch," Luce muttered, looking toward the main lobby of the motel in disbelief. He was actually here. Luce strode that way, pausing outside and glancing through the window with the florescent vacancy sign shining from it.

Serah sat behind a desk, humming to herself, her feet kicked up and a magazine on her lap. Abaddon lurked nearby, stone cold silent as he watched her. He was invisible to the human eye—should be invisible—but there was no telling where Serah was concerned. After all, she'd seen *him*.

Don.

Luce silently called out to him, the name ringing loud and clear in his mind. Abaddon immediately shifted position, glancing toward the window a second before he vanished from the room. He popped up in the parking lot, a grin lighting up the angel's face as he regarded him. "Luce, good to see you again."

Luce glared at him. "What do you think you're doing?"

Abaddon raised his eyebrows. "I'm just hanging around."

"With Serah?" Luce asked incredulously. "You thought that was wise? That I'd be okay with that?"

Abaddon raised his hands defensively. "Relax, brother. She couldn't see me."

"Are you sure about that?" Luce asked.

Abaddon's gaze darted toward the motel with confusion before he looked back at Luce. "Yeah, positive. She had no idea I was there. I didn't show myself to her."

"But you have," Luce said, stepping toward him. "You've shown yourself."

Abaddon laughed lightly, shrugging a shoulder as if it weren't a big deal. "She needed some help. That's what Guardians do, right? Help the humans."

"She's not just a human," Luce said. "She's different, and you know it. Stay away from her."

"Ah, come on... don't be like that."

Luce got right up in his face. "Don't make me tell you again, Don. I don't take well to being disregarded."

Abaddon's posture stiffened, his playful expression fading away. Gone was the old friend Luce once knew, the angel's eyes darkening a shade, the blue deepening to a peculiar purple. It was a color Luce knew well... the next step from there was black and then red, the eyes that had stared back at Luce every time he caught sight of his reflection in a spans of crystal clear water or a sliver of glass down in the pit. They were the eyes of evil, the eyes of someone who had gone over the edge and allowed themselves to be consumed by wrath.

Blue was pure; blue was the color of benevolence.

When sin crept in, taking over every cell in the body, darkening the soul, the world turned bright red.

Abaddon was just a few steps away from the point of no return.

"Careful, Don," Luce warned. "Don't do anything you'll regret."

Abaddon scoffed. "I regret nothing."

"Nothing?" Luce asked. "You don't regret double-crossing me? Turning your back on me? Leaving me to face the consequences alone? What about sinning, huh? You don't regret that anymore?"

Leaning forward, Abaddon narrowed his eyes indignantly, a mocking smirk turning the corner of his lips. "Nothing."

With a loud pop of static, the angel was gone, leaving Luce alone in the parking lot. Before he could react, a loud gasp echoed through the air around him. He quickly turned his head toward the sound, tensing when he saw Serah standing at the glass door, looking out. Her eyes were fixed straight to him. While he couldn't see his reflection in the glass, knowing nobody else would know he was there, he could tell she saw him.

Fuck.

She squeezed her eyes shut tightly and counted to ten. Although she whispered, the words barely a breath, Luce could hear her. She reopened her eyes, meeting his, and blinked rapidly before doing it again.

And again.

She expected him to disappear.

He probably should've disappeared, vanishing while her eyes were closed so she'd think he wasn't real again, but he couldn't.

Michael was wrong. He wasn't a coward. But he was a pathetic son of a bitch who couldn't bear to keep letting go of her.

Shaking his head, he laughed dryly to himself before turning toward the door. Serah's eyes widened when they broke from his gaze, drifting down to his chest as she gasped again. He glanced down, realizing he wasn't wearing his shirt, and although the wound he'd inflicted on himself had started to slowly heal, blood covered his chest.

The door to the motel thrust open and Serah stepped out into the darkened parking lot.

"Hello?" she called out. "Are you okay?"

"I'm fine." His voice was quiet, barely loud enough for her to hear. "Go back inside."

"You're bleeding," she said, ignoring his command as she slowly approached. "Do you need some help? Do you need me to call someone?"

"I'm fine," he said again. "Go back inside."

Once more, she ignored him, closing the rest of the distance between them. Lucifer exhaled loudly, the scent of her swarming him when he inhaled again. Flowers. She smelled like fucking flowers. How he missed that...

Before he could react, her hands were on him, touching him, one hand grasping his bicep while the other reached for his chest. He hissed when her fingertips connected with the bare skin. It was scarcely a graze, but he felt it deep down like a jolt of electricity. He damn near shivered.

"Oh God, I didn't hurt you, did I?" she asked, yanking her hand back away. "You're hurt. Geez, you're burning up! I'm so sorry. I just... come on, come inside. I'll get you some help."

"I'm fine," he said for the third time, but it was pointless. She yanked on his arm, and although he was strong enough to resist her, he didn't. He let her drag him toward the motel, heading inside with her. She shoved him toward a chair and he plopped down in it, shaking his head as she scrambled around for something, disappearing into a side room briefly.

She returned with a wet rag and immediately started blotting the blood from his skin. Lucifer sat as still as possible, watching her with disbelief as she rambled on and on. "What happened to you? Did you get cut or something? Did somebody do this to you? It looks like something, like a pattern or something... it's starting to heal already, though. How long ago did it happen? Does it hurt? What happened to you?"

The same questions asked in a loop.

Lucifer didn't answer a single one of them, just staring at her, stunned to be this close again. She was utterly beautiful... flawless creamy skin and the deepest brown eyes. Blue was pure, sure, like the sky above, but her brown eyes were as rich and warm as the earth. There was something comforting about them. He once envied the humans because they were given the Earth, but looking at her, he wondered if maybe Paradise was to be found in a person and not a place.

"What is this?" she asked, running the rag around the wound. "It's some shape, like a triangle with a graph, and hook and a 'V'. I've, uh... I've seen this somewhere before. Who did this to you? What is it?"

Reaching up, Luce palmed her cheek, his touch making her eyes flutter before she met his gaze again.

"I'm fine," he said. "You should've stayed inside."

She stared into his eyes, her anxiety fading as her shoulders relaxed. She paused the rag near his collarbone, the only movement the rise and fall of her chest, the blink of her eyes, the beat of her heart.

Thump.

Thump.

Thump.

Lucifer listened to the steady rhythm, relishing the sound of it.

"Tell me I'm not crazy," she whispered.

"You're not crazy."

"Tell me you're real."

"I'm real."

"Really real?"

He cracked a smile, his thumb gently stroking her cheek. "As real as you."

"Who are you?" she asked tentatively, biting down on her bottom lip. "Where did you come from?"

He laughed dryly. "That's a long story."

"I have time."

"Not enough," he responded. "Never enough time."

For her, anyway. Luce had all the time in the world. Eternity. But her life would be barely the blink of an eye in the grand scheme of things, and then she'd go to Heaven, and stay in Heaven. And he'd still be here.

Or back down there.

"I have to be crazy," she whispered, more to herself than anyone as she pulled away from him. She plopped down in a chair beside him, tossing the rag down on the desk. She ran her hands down her face, shielding herself as she lowered her head. "You're not real. I'm dreaming again. Wake up, Sarah. Time to wake up."

"Serah," he whispered, pulling her hands away

from her face. "Your name's Serah. And you're not crazy... not the crazy you're thinking, anyway."

Crazy for falling for him, maybe.

Eyes wide, she met his gaze again. "You know my name?"

"I do."

"You knew me?" she asked, hesitating before clarifying, "You know me?"

"Yes."

"Who am I?"

"That's another long story."

She sighed with frustration, whispering her name to herself, like she was trying it out. Luce watched her mouth move, sounding it out. Fuck, how he wanted to kiss those lips...

"Were you there?" she asked, the question distracting Luce from thoughts of kissing her before he slipped up and acted on the impulse. Who knew he had any sort of self-control?

"Was I where?"

"In the street," she said. "The day I woke up. Were you there? Because I remember you... I remember your eyes."

He nodded slowly. "I was there."

"What happened to me?" she asked. *Such a loaded*

120

question. Luce was about to say it was a long story when she cut back in. "Please, I don't care how long it takes, I want to know. I *need* to know."

He considered it for a moment, considered making up some lie, some boring, believable story that would soothe her curiosity, but he couldn't. Lying used to come so easy for him, and it still did, but he couldn't lie to her about this.

"It was a mistake," he said quietly. "You went somewhere you shouldn't have gone, got caught up in someone else's fight, and you ended up hurt because of it."

"How?" she asked. "How did I get hurt?"

Luce was quiet for a moment, staring at her, as he finally pulled his hands away, his fingertips leaving her skin. "You trusted someone you shouldn't have ever trusted."

"Who?"

"Someone who nearly destroyed you."

She shook her head. "Do you always speak so cryptically?"

He shrugged a shoulder. He was trying to convince her she wasn't crazy. Any more details than that and she was liable to check herself into a mental institution.

The devil tricked you to trigger the apocalypse, and then he stuck a knife through your chest, but I swear it was out of love.

"Have you considered maybe you're better off not knowing?" he asked. "That maybe there's a reason you don't remember any of it?"

"What if it was you?" she asked. "How would you feel?"

He laughed dryly. "I'd give just about anything to have a clean slate."

"But I just... I want to know who I am. I want to know where I came from. Do I have a family? Friends? Does anybody care? Does anyone miss me, or remember me, or even think about me?"

"I do," he said quietly.

"And who are you?" she asked, cutting him off when he tried to respond right away. "I know you said it's a long story, but can I get the short version? At least a name? Something?"

He considered it for a moment. "Luce."

"Luce," she repeated, brow furrowing. "Is that short for something?"

"Yes."

He didn't elaborate. She didn't press the matter. Her eyes bore into his as her mouth again moved, sounding out his name this time, a small smile playing on her lips. Fuck, he *really* wanted to kiss her...

Her eyes eventually left his, drifting along him, scanning his face and his bare chest before meeting his gaze again. She quirked an eyebrow, holding her hand out. "Well, Luce, apparently I'm Serah."

Lucifer reached out and took her hand, holding it in his. "I know."

"Lucky for you, my memory is shot, which means you're a clean slate to me. I'm learning from scratch here, trying to make sense of the world again, but I have a question that I think might clear some things up."

He hesitated. "I'm listening."

"How in the world did you heal so quickly?"

He immediately looked down, realizing the wound on his chest was now gone. All that was left was the faint circular scar from the burn of a Heavenly blade. "The wound was superficial."

"And the round scar?" she asked. "Where did *that* come from?"

"Can't really say."

"Pity," she said, tugging on the neck of her shirt and pulling it down to expose a patch of skin. "Because I have one of those marks, too."

Lucifer stared at the scar on her chest. His would

123

fade by tomorrow as he fully regenerated, but she was human now. Marks on humans remained. Hers became permanent the moment he took her wings.

He wasn't sure what to say, so he said nothing, pulling away from her entirely to stand up. "I really shouldn't be here, Serah."

He turned to leave, ignoring her feeble protest asking him to stay. He shouldn't be there; he shouldn't be talking to her, or touching her. The truth would only hurt her in the end.

As soon as he stepped outside, away from her eyes, he zapped away and landed on the street outside of the old bar he'd tracked Abaddon to before. He tried to sense his old friend, not done with their conversation, but Abaddon's essence faded as soon as he appeared.

He knew that game.

The angel was evading him.

Luce.

The name was peculiar, yet somehow familiar; like it was a name Serah knew intimately, one she had spoken many times before. *Luce.*

It repeatedly rolled through her thoughts, springing off the tip of her tongue after having lingered there for months. It made sense, relatively speaking, considering nothing about the entire situation was truly understandable.

She wondered if she was dreaming again.

In the blink of an eye, her visitor was up out of the chair, his words not registering with her until he was almost to the door. *I shouldn't be here.* "Hang on," she called out. "Stay, please!"

She jumped up, running to the door when he headed outside, stepping out not ten seconds after him to find the dark parking lot completely empty.

Gone.

"Wait!" she yelled, looking around. He couldn't have gotten far. "Come back!"

"Looking for someone?"

She jumped at the unexpected voice, startlingly close. A man stood on the corner a mere few feet away. How hadn't she seen him until now? It wasn't Luce, but when he took a step closer, recognition dawned. She'd met him before, once, not long ago: the guy who had carried her groceries for her.

Don.

"Uh, yeah," she said quickly. "Did you see someone come by here?"

"No," he said. "Should I have?"

"I, uh... I don't know." Shaking her head, she scanned the parking lot once more, seeing no sign of him anywhere. It was like he'd vanished into thin air again. *Typical.* "I guess not."

Sighing, she turned around and stepped back inside the lobby of the motel, trying to shake off the peculiar feeling crawling across her skin, the tingling along her spine. She could sense the man as he stepped in behind her.

"Can I help you with something?" she asked, grabbing the bloody rag from the desk, the only evidence she had that her visitor had been real.

"I was hoping so."

"Do you need a room?" she asked, raising her eyebrows curiously. "We have some vacancy."

"No, I'm afraid I don't need that kind of help."

"What kind of help do you need?"

"The kind I think only you can help me with."

He grinned, a sly sort of grin that made Serah's defenses prickle. She turned away from him, carefully folding the rag up and laying it in the hamper for laundry in the morning. "I'm not sure how I can help you, mister, but I—"

She turned back around, cutting off mid-sentence when she realized she was alone. She stared at the spot he'd just occupied, that sensation inside of her growing, her stomach twisting, heart thumping wildly. She hadn't heard the door open, hadn't heard him leave, but he wasn't there anymore.

I'm losing it.

After a quick glance around the lobby, ensuring she was in fact alone, she retook her seat at the desk, trying to ignore the queasiness building inside of her. There was something very wrong, something happening that she couldn't understand. Absently, her hand drifted up to her chest and she rubbed the scar through her shirt.

She had a feeling it might be the key to everything.

Three

The one-story house was quaint, white with blue
shutters, located in a quiet neighborhood toward the
south end of Chorizon, just a few blocks away from
the local elementary school. The *'for rent'* sign still
stuck out of the shabby patch of grass out front, but
Serah had already signed her name on the dotted
line, making her the official tenant.

Or *part* of her name.

What she was pretty sure was her name now,
anyway.

Her boss, Gilda, knew the owners and had
helped her rent the house, despite her lack of
history, and credit, and whatever else it was people
needed to get a place of their own.

It was hers now — for the next year, at least.

It was a warm summer morning, the sun
shining brightly already at only nine o'clock. Serah
stepped out of her house wearing a light summer
dress and a pair of white flip-flops, her long hair
pulled up off her neck. She had no plans, nowhere

to go or nothing to do, so she just ventured around town as usual, wandering streets she'd wandered every day the past few months. It was fairly busy for being a Sunday, the streets bustling as people made their way to church. There were plenty of churches around town, from elaborate cathedrals and quaint little buildings that looked like barns, but Serah was continually drawn to the community center in town instead of those places.

She'd sat it on church a few times—it seemed like the thing to do here, and something about it always felt familiar, like she was at home sitting on the grungy little folding metal chair in the recently remodeled community center. She knew the scripture, knew the stories the preacher recounted, a few times almost chiming in to correct the man when he misinterpreted something. She forced herself to remain silent, though, merely listening. After all, he was the authority on the subject.

What did *she* know?

She'd only just learned her own name.

The room was half-filled today, the usual visitors occupying the chairs. Serah sat at the front and listened as the preacher talked about the great flood. She doodled in the margins of her brand new bible—a housewarming present from Gilda, which was really just one of the extras they ordered for the nightstands in the motel rooms. Her mind drifted... she knew this story like the back of her hand... as she absently drew a peculiar geometric pattern, a rendering of the mark she'd seen not long ago. Upside down triangle that evolved into hooks, an 'x' slashed through it, with a letter V beneath it all. She drew it so many times the past week, trying to find significance in the shapes, that she could probably produce it in her sleep. What was it? What did it mean?

Why had it been slashed into his skin?

It left a lingering mark, a mark that she too carried.

Had that mark once been on her skin, too?

When service was over, she stood to leave when the preacher stopped her. "You know, some believe it's wrong to write in bibles. Revelations tells us not to add or subtract from God's words."

She smiled softly. "That's not meant to be taken literally."

He raised his eyebrows. "No?"

"This is just a book," she said, holding up her bible. "It's just paper and ink. It's the medium, not the meaning."

"That's one way to look at it," he said, holding up his own bible with a smile, the page it was on highlighted and scribbled all over. "I tend to agree."

"Besides, I wasn't writing," she said. "I was drawing."

"Oh? What were you drawing?"

Serah flipped open to the page she was doodling on and held it up.

The preacher's expression fell slowly as he gazed at it. "Can't say I have one of those in my book. Can't say I'd ever put one in my book."

Serah's brow furrowed. "Have you seen it before?"

"Of course," he said, closing his bible before clearing his throat, turning away from her. His warm eyes suddenly felt icy. "Excuse me."

He started to walk away when she stepped in front of him in the aisle. "Wait a second... where have you seen this before?"

He only paused for a fraction of a second. "It's one of the marks of Satan, one he bore before his fall."

Serah just stood there as the man scurried away. *Satan?* Shaking her head with disbelief, she looked down at the drawing before closing her bible again.

He must be mistaken.

Sighing, she walked out of the community center and strolled down the street, heading back home.

The neighborhood was alive with activity when she arrived, people gardening, children playing, others enjoying the sunshine. Some boys played basketball in the street a few houses down, the man across the street mowing his grass. Serah approached her house, carrying her bible under her arm, when a red ball suddenly flew right past her feet, nearly tripping her as it came to a stop in her front yard.

Brow furrowing, she reached down and picked it up when a squeaky voice cut through the air behind her. "Are you lost some more?"

Serah turned around, seeing a small child with mousy brown hair and wide eyes. She vaguely recognized her, remembering the encounter outside the elementary school not long ago. "No, I've been found," she said, smiling warmly as she held up the ball. "Yours?"

The little girl nodded enthusiastically, taking the ball from her. "Do you still got the amnesia?"

"I do," Serah said, surprised the child remembered

the incident. Nicki, she recalled her name. She had a father named Nicholas and a mother named Samantha. "They think I'll always have it."

"So you don't remember nothing?"

"I remember some things," she said. "I remember meeting you, for instance."

Nicki lit up excitedly.

"Oh, and I remember my name now," she said. "Or well... somebody told me my name. It's Serah."

"I'm still Nicki," the girl said. "Do you live here now?"

"I do."

"Mr. Johnson used to live here. He wasn't so nice. He got mad when my ball went on his grass, 'cause mama said he didn't like kids. But then he got married to a beauty queen and moved away. Mama called them Beauty and the Beast, because he was hairy and mean, but the Beast was a good guy so I think he was really Gaston." Nicki paused to take a breath. "Oh! Maybe that's what you need!"

Serah's eyes widened. "A Beast?"

"No, silly, a frog!"

Serah stared at her incredulously. "A frog?"

"Don't you read fairy tales? You kiss a frog and he becomes a prince!"

Serah had to wonder if maybe she wasn't the only crazy one. "And how will a frog prince help me?"

Nicki shrugged. "It always helps the princesses in the stories."

Before Serah could respond, a female voice cut through the air from the house next door. Looking up, Serah saw a woman on the front steps, a petite brunette with a bulging stomach. Her hands rested on her belly as she watched them, her expression kind. "Nicki, time for lunch!"

"That's my mama," Nicki said. "I gotta go. I'm glad you were found!"

Nicki ran off before Serah could say anything. She watched the girl disappear into the house, smiling softly. Something about her innocence felt so familiar, so comforting.

Lucifer stood in the quiet parking lot, his back to the old motel. It was nearing dawn, the sky still dark, only a faint orange glow spilling out on the horizon. The town was quiet, most everyone asleep.

Everyone except for *her*.

She was still working.

He wasn't sure why he was here. He hadn't even thought about it. He tracked Abaddon around the godforsaken world, jumping from place to place, before ultimately ending up right back where he started.

He was weak.

She was tempting.

Lust was his favorite sin, but he was beginning to dislike its counterpart, the one called greed. Because he was insatiable, especially when it came to her. He wanted more, and more, and more. It was never enough.

He wondered if it ever would be.

It would have to be.

He knew he should stay away, that he *needed* to stay away, to keep his distance, but he couldn't. As much as he tried, he always ended up back here. Warnings be damned...

The door to the motel jingled, soft footsteps starting through the parking lot. Six o'clock in the morning, Lucifer gathered. Probably not a minute later. Humans were good with time. Peculiar things, how they monitored every hour, minute, second, scheduling themselves to utilize every bit of time they're given. He supposed it made sense, when you're granted only a few decades on earth. Sixty, seventy, eighty years, if you're lucky.

He'd squandered more time than that in a long card game.

Time for him always meant nothing. A thousand years was a breeze. Six thousand was barely enough time to get amply pissed off about being trapped in the pit. He never realized how much time he'd wasted until he was staring down a ticking clock, his time with her running short.

It caused something to materialize inside of him when he let that thought simmer, something he'd never felt before. Guilt.

Guilt, because there was only one to blame for the human's short lives, and contrary to popular belief, it wasn't Eve.

"Coffee?"

He closed his eyes briefly, letting the sound of her voice wash through him, before slowly turning around. Serah stood just a few feet away, eyes fixed directly on him. Although he knew, deep down, she saw him, his eyes still flitted around the parking lot, certain there had to be somebody—*anybody*—else that she was speaking to. But they were alone.

"Coffee?" he asked. "What about it?"

"Do you want to get some?"

His brow furrowed. "For what?"

"To drink," she said hesitantly. "And, I don't know, I thought maybe we could hang out and... talk, I guess."

Coffee. To drink. To hang out. To talk.

With her.

Lucifer stared at her for a moment. Logic told him to turn her away, but that goddamned greed manifested, begging him to take every second of her short life she would offer him. She was only given so many, after all. If he said no to these, she may not offer him any more.

"It doesn't have to be coffee," she said tentatively. "I don't even like coffee. We can get some breakfast at the diner down the street. I mean, everybody has to eat, right?"

"Right," he said, drawing out the word. Except he wasn't an *'everybody'*... he was a nobody, or a somebody, depending on how you looked at it. A nobody who didn't exist, not really, not here, but saying yes meant he had to be a somebody. He'd have to break his rule, the one rule he set for himself long, long ago, the one rule that he swore he'd never break. The one he never wanted to break. Not until this moment, anyway.

He'd have to show himself to the humans.

She could see him, but he was still out of sight to the others, and he couldn't have her looking certifiably insane, seen in public hanging out and talking to someone who wasn't there.

As if she could read his mind, she chimed back in, her voice a pleading whisper. "Please? I'm not crazy... I'm *not*."

"I know you're not," he said. "And yes... we can get breakfast."

Her shoulders seemed to sag with relief, a small smile playing on her lips at his response. "Great, uh... well, come on."

She motioned with her head in the direction of the diner before turning away from him. The moment her back was to him, he gave a quick glance around the parking lot, making sure not another living soul was around, before he dropped his guard completely. The air around him sparked, as if consumed by static, his body tingling with a soft glow as he let himself be visible.

Serah glanced back at him, to make sure he was coming, her footsteps wavering, a look of surprise coming over her face as he strode forward.

"What?" he asked, raising his eyebrows in question as he stared at her, falling into step right beside her.

"Oh, uh, nothing," she said, a soft blush warming her cheeks. "It's just... I don't know. Strange."

"What's strange?"

"You kind of looked like you were glowing a second ago," she said, the blush deepening. "Must've been the light or something."

"Must have," he replied, surprised she saw that, although he shouldn't have been. She'd been seeing and sensing things she shouldn't have all along.

They walked quietly to the diner, the sun rising, the orange glow expanding and covering everything in a soft light. They stood so close their arms nearly brushed against one another, but Luce made sure not to touch her. When she moved, he moved, shifting a fraction of an inch away, like they were magnets facing the wrong way. He could feel it, though—the pull toward her, the tingle along his skin that reminded him of being bathed in her Grace.

Fuck, he did her wrong.

Over and over.

Don't let me do it again.

The diner was brightly lit, but only a few people sat inside at this hour. Serah paused when she reached the door, scowling at a small sign in the window.

No shirt

No shoes

No service

She turned to look at him, and Lucifer knew what she was going to say before she even said anything. He had a shirt, yes, but his feet were bare.

Her eyes shifted to the sidewalk as she took stock of his feet. "Are you homeless?"

Silence surrounded them for a moment. Luce could tell she was anxious to ask that, could sense her apprehension, but her words came off humorous to him. He laughed, unable to contain himself.

Because yes, he was homeless, relatively speaking. He sure as fuck had nowhere to call *home*.

"Go on inside and sit down," he said, reaching past her to grab the door, opening it. "I'll be back in just a minute."

She hesitated again, as if she thought he might be bailing on her, but chose to believe him after a moment. Offering a smile, she stepped inside the diner, as Luce let go of the door.

J.M. Darhower

The second he was certain nobody was looking, he zapped away, out of sight, apparating just around the block. In a jiffy, a pair of black boots materialized on his feet. He zapped right back, appearing once more in the same spot as before. He opened the door, stepping inside the diner, just as Serah was sliding into a booth. She glanced up at him, wide-eyed, when he slipped into the booth across from her. "You're back?"

"Yes," he said. "I said it would only take a minute. I didn't take longer than that, did I?"

"Uh, no," she said, gaping at him. "I mean, I don't even think that was a minute. You were just standing out there, and I just sat down, and..." She bent over, looking under the table, before meeting his eyes again. "You have shoes on!"

"Yes," he said again.

"How did you do that? That's impossible! I can't even put on flip-flops that fast when they're right in front of me!"

He shrugged a shoulder, making a mental note to slow down if ever this happened again. Humans, for being so obsessed with time, certainly did everything leisurely.

She was still gaping at him when the waitress

appeared, sliding two menus on the table in front of them. Lucifer picked one up, having absolutely no interest in food. He'd never tried to eat it, never cared to try it. He was certain he could, though. After all, it was all their Father's creation. His body would merely absorb it, converting it to energy.

"What can I get you to drink?" the waitress asked.

"Orange juice," Serah said right away.

Lucifer continued to just stare at his menu.

"For you, darling?" the waitress asked.

It wasn't until Serah whispered his name that he realized the woman was talking to him.

"Luce?" Serah said. "To drink?"

"Water," he responded, staring at Serah. "And an apple to eat."

Her brow furrowed. "Just an apple?"

"Yes," he confirmed. "An apple."

It wasn't on the menu, but he was certain a place like this had one.

She blinked a few times, shrugging it off, as she took his menu and placed it on top of hers. She ordered for the both of them... just an apple for him, while she ordered a vast array of things.

The waitress wandered away then, taking much too long to leave them in peace. Serah regarded him warily, but remained quiet until after their drinks were brought to the table. Sticking a straw in her glass, she took a sip, eyes never leaving his. "Can I ask you something, Luce?"

He couldn't help but smile at the sound of his name on her lips. She'd said it twice now since they sat down. "You can ask whatever you'd like."

"How do you do it?"

"Do what?"

"Disappear," she said, her voice quiet. "One second you're right there, and then you're gone. It's like... magic. You're not a wizard, are you?"

He laughed. "What do you know about wizards?"

She shrugged, her face flushing as she averted her eyes, as if embarrassed. "I read books."

"Do you?"

"Yes."

"Just because you read it doesn't make it real."

"I know," she said, fidgeting in her seat. "I know wizards aren't real, but sometimes I question whether you are, too. Until that waitress spoke to you, I half-expected her to not see you. Nobody else ever seems to... and I just wonder why that is. It's unnatural."

Intuitive. Luce stared at her, surprised by her bluntness. She laid her cards all out on the table and asked to see his hand, a hand he wasn't quite ready to show. "Unnatural."

"Yes," she said. "Like... not normal."

Luce watched in silence as she took a sip of her orange juice, her eyes peeled to him.

"That's because I'm not," he said. "I'm not normal."

"What are you then?"

He laughed dryly. "An abomination, apparently."

She rolled her eyes, like he'd been joking. *If she only knew...*

Neither of them spoke again until after their food arrived—two plates for Serah, a lone apple for Luce. He picked it up, rolling it around in his palm as he stared at it. It looked quite similar to the one Eve ate that day in the garden, the skin the same shade of deep red.

"So," Serah hedged as she started to eat. "How is it you knew me?"

"Long story."

"Shorten it."

Luce let out a deep sigh. "Work."

Her eyes widened as she slowly chewed a bite, staring at him. Luce realized after a moment that she expected him to go on.

Apparently that answer had been too short.

"We were working on different sides," he explained, trying to word is so she'd understand without actually telling her the truth about it. It was a fine line to walk, one he was sure he was going to fuck up. "It was your job to try to bring me around to your side."

"Different sides of what?" she asked. "What do you do for work, Luce?"

"Nothing now," he said. "I was, uh... *let go*."

"Okay, so what *did* you do?"

"Babysat."

That answer made her laugh, again like she thought he was joking, but he'd meant it. It was glorified babysitting down in the pit.

"I supervised the imprisoned," he said. "And you worked for those who make it their job to keep the world safe, to make sure the bad was kept locked away."

"So you were like, a warden," she said. "And I was, what? One of the powers that be?"

"Uh..." Luce laughed at her wording. She

146

couldn't have been more right if she tried. "Basically."

"Interesting," she said. "And did I sway you to our side?"

"Debatable," he said. "You put up a strong argument, though, which is a testament of my being here."

"Wow." She ate some more in silence, the air between them comfortable. Luce just watched her, not interrupting, saying nothing. Eventually she pushed a plate aside and cleared her throat. "You know none of that makes any sense to me, right? I'm still just as confused."

"I know you are," he said quietly. "If it's any consolation, I'm confused, too."

"Okay, new tactic," she said, pointing at him with her fork. "Since my memory's shot and you said you'd give anything to have a clean slate, why don't we start there?"

"Okay."

"Okay, good." She nodded firmly. "So tell me something."

"What?"

"Anything," she said. "Just tell me something, whatever you'd like me to know about you... no matter what it is. We're starting from scratch."

"Uh..." Luce wasn't quite sure what to say. She was taking this all in stride, way better than he expected her to take it.

"I'll start," she said after a moment, turning her eyes back to her plate as she shifted some potatoes around with her fork. "I love the smell of fresh-cut grass, but it makes me sneeze."

Luce smiled at her, a little surprised by the random nonsensical declaration, but he wasn't at all shocked by the information. She'd been fascinated with the concept of smelling. "I love fresh air."

"Is that why you spend a lot of time outside?"

"How do you know I do that?"

"Because I spend a lot of time outside, and I see you almost every day."

"It's one of the reasons."

The other being he had nowhere else to be, but he kept that to himself for now.

"Well, as you can see, I love food," she said motioning toward her plates. "When I woke up, I felt like I hadn't eaten in *forever*. People always say that hospital food is horrible. When they find out I spent weeks in the hospital, that's the first thing they say— that the food must've been horrible. But I couldn't get enough of it."

"What was it like being in the hospital?" Luce asked.

"Horrible," she said. "Minus the food, anyway. They couldn't find anything wrong with me physically, so they said it had to be psychological, but the psychiatrist said I wasn't a danger to anyone, so I was free to go."

"So you left."

"So I left," she agreed, "and here I am."

She finished eating in silence as the waitress returned with the bill, casting Luce a peculiar look. Serah glanced at the check and pulled out some money, tossing it down on the table. A sinking feeling settled in the pit of Luce's stomach. He hadn't thought this through at all. He knew little about the usage of money, but he knew human customs after years of observing them from the pit.

He knew he should offer to pay.

He just wasn't sure how to go about it.

Before he could try to materialize some money, or offer to pay her back or something, Serah was sliding out of her seat. "Ready?"

"Sure."

Luce stood up as she strutted passed him on her way to the door. Hesitating, Luce glanced at the apple in his hand before slowly bringing it to his lips.

He bit down on it.

It was crisp, with a sharp sort of taste, intense and sweet. He chewed for a moment before swallowing, shrugging as he tossed the apple down on the table, discarding it.

It wasn't half-bad, but it certainly wasn't worth losing your head over.

Something happened that afternoon in the garden.

As Eve consumed the apple, plucking another from the Tree of Knowledge to share with Adam, there was a shift in the air. A chill rolled down Lucifer's spine, crawling across his skin. He shivered from the unexpected sensation, blinking his eyes a few times, watching as redness crept along Eve's bare flesh. It was as if the blood had moved to the surface, flushing her a shade of pink, a sensation he felt echoing in him.

Feeling.

"What have you done?"

His Father's voice rang out right behind him, low

and desolate. Luce smiled with satisfaction, turning his head, expecting to see anger targeted at His new children for disobeying, but His focus was on the Archangel instead. His eyes were full of pain, the same sort of pain Luce had seen in Adam's face the day he'd been injured.

"Your children," Luce said, "have been seduced by evil."

"If it was evil that seduced them," He asked, "what does that make you?"

The question stalled Luce. He just stared at his Father as He turned away.

The Wrath of God was felt for the first time that afternoon. The sunny sky was awash with darkness, the first storm descending upon the earth. Luce stood there, still leaning against the tree, and watched as the humans were punished.

Pain and heartache were cast upon them, condemning them to struggle for their disobedience. Stripped of innocence, their hearts were now tainted, hearts that no longer would beat for an eternity. They squandered His gift, He said, so He was taking it back. They'd no longer live forever. Someday, and soon, their hearts would give out on them.

Lucifer felt the smallest hint of satisfaction when

they were cast out of the garden, these new mortals banned from Paradise. They couldn't be trusted not to eat from the Tree of Life, lest they get the idea to try to steal their immortality back. The unrest went on all day, lighting flashing and thunder rumbling, rain pouring down in waves. When it finally calmed down, the air in the garden settling, Lucifer and his Father were left all alone.

The anger faded, and as He turned to Lucifer, the Archangel once more saw His desolation.

"Why?" He asked quietly. "Why would you do it?"

"I wanted you to see your children weren't perfect," Lucifer said. "I wanted you to see they could be corrupted, that they could be infected by evil."

"I saw," He said, staring right at Lucifer. "I saw the corruption. I saw the evil. I saw it all, my son, and it started with you."

"It's not much." Serah's voice was a soft whisper as she hurriedly picked up a few stray things from her living room: a blanket covering the couch, an empty glass on the end table, and a pair of shoes discarded on the floor. "Sorry about the mess."

She cast a nervous smile toward the front door. Was it a mess? She wasn't sure. She'd certainly seen worse in rooms at the motel.

Luce stood in the open doorway, blocking the sunlight behind him, like he was afraid to come in any further. Was this a mistake? She was thinking it might be. She saw the man around town, always watching her, and after two strange conversations with him she invites him to her home.

He came along willingly, but now that they were here, he looked uncomfortable.

"So, uh, you can come in, if you want," she said, gesturing with her hands. "Make yourself at home."

He cracked a smile as he carefully shut the door behind him and strolled into the living room. His newly acquired boots were heavy against the wooden floor, echoing off the vacant walls. Serah could feel her heart pounding harder along to the sound. Luce regarded her for a moment, just standing there in front of her.

"This is dangerous," he said quietly, his eyes flickering around the room. "You should be careful who you invite into your home."

"I am," she whispered. "I never have before... nobody else has ever... you know."

Did he know?

She didn't even really know.

She didn't have family; she didn't have friends.

She had nobody to invite inside except for him.

Who was he? What was he to her? All she had was a name and a vague story, most of which she couldn't be certain was true. But she had an unshakable feeling about him, her gut instinct putting her at ease, drawing her to him. It was simultaneously feeling safe while having her nerves frayed.

His eyes alone set her insides ablaze.

The blue looked dark as midnight at the moment, a twinkle in his eyes like they held all the stars in his gaze. He had a solar system inside of him, a universe of secrets Serah yearned to explore.

She wasn't sure why, or how, but she felt like she'd been there before. The closer he stepped to her, the deeper the feeling grew. Familiar... *so familiar*.

He felt like a part of her.

Goosebumps coated her skin, from the top of her head to the tip of her toes. He smelled like peppermint with a hint of sulfur, like someone had struck a match not long ago. He stopped right in front of her, leaning down to stare her in the eyes, his expression dead serious.

His lips were a mere breath away.

"You feel it, don't you?" he asked, his voice gritty, barely a whisper. "You still feel it."

What? She wanted to ask, the words on the tip of her tongue, but they wouldn't come out. *What is this I'm feeling between us?*

The back of his hand brushed against her flushed cheek, sending sparks across her skin. Her breath hitched, heart skipping a beat at the sensation. Maybe it was her imagination, but she could've sworn his eyes blackened, a growl vibrating his chest.

"I can tell you do," he said, inching closer. "You may not remember, but it's still there."

What is it?

She yearned to know.

Luce's nose brushed against hers before he tilted his head. Her heart raced frantically. His lips lightly touched hers, barely a kiss, a soft graze, but it ignited something inside of her, rekindling an extinguished flame.

He deepened the kiss, groaning into her mouth. She inhaled sharply, flashes of him assaulting her out of nowhere.

A crystal clear lake. Laughter. An embrace. A table. Cracked marble. Him on top of her, inside of her, again and again. Violent and vicious, passionate and out of control. A flash of fire. A flash of screaming. Vibrant red eyes staring at her.

Gasping, Serah shoved against him, moving away. Luce froze, watching her incredulously, as she tried to catch her breath. She stared at him, her body vibrating, a twinge of fear coursing through her.

Luce's expression softened, his eyes melting to an icy blue, the same shade as the lake. She'd been there... *they'd* been there. "What... what was that?"

He was still for a moment, stoic, his voice hesitant. "Why don't you tell me?"

She rattled off what she saw—a lake, a table, the flames. She said his eyes had been blood red, eerie as they glared her way. Luce remained still, not reacting, waiting until she finished.

As soon as she quieted down, he stepped toward her, reaching out and cupping her cheek. She didn't move away, didn't flinch. She leaned into his touch involuntarily.

"I wish I could tell you everything you want to know," he said, "but then my slate wouldn't be clean anymore."

Part of her yearned to tell him that didn't matter, but she kept that to herself. Luce leaned down again, placing a light peck on her lips, then another, and another, each softer than the first.

Serah's eyes fluttered closed.

Pulling back, he whispered, just an inch from her lips. "I have to go."

She felt a soft breeze, a tingle along her skin. Her eyes snapped open, finding the room empty.

Luce was gone.

She was alone again.

"Truce?"

Lucifer glared at the scruffy looking Guardian. Abaddon had both hands raised in mock surrender, an amused smirk tugging his lips.

Truce? No truce. There would never be a truce. There is no draw—you either win or you lose. He'd had many angels toss that word at him only to be laughed away, but Luce found nothing funny today.

He'd sensed his old friend's presence outside Serah's house, lurking around in the neighborhood. Luce had caught him off guard, cornering him in the street.

"What are you doing here?" Luce asked.

"Curiosity."

"You seem to be full of that lately."

"What can I say?" He shrugged noncommittally. "It's a curious world we exist in, and I can't help but wonder how much Serah knows. Does she realize she's living beside her Heavenly brother? Does she have any idea?"

"No," Luce said. "She doesn't remember anything."

"Except for you," Abaddon corrected him. "She oddly remembers you. That was a nice little show you put on in there, by the way. Tell me something, old friend... does she taste as sweet as a mortal as she did as an angel? Or was kissing her just a part of your game?"

"What game?"

"Whatever game it is you're playing."

"She's not a part of any game," Luce said.

Abaddon nodded, slowly lowering his hands as his smile fell. "So your attempt to play house with a mortal is genuine? How long do you think He will tolerate that? Do you know how many angels your brother had to smite in your absence because they tried to intermingle? Too many. You can't keep her, Lucifer. He's not going to let you."

Luce's skin tingled, the hair on his arms standing on end at those words as the anger he'd tried to control started simmering inside of him. Letting go of Serah was impossible. He'd tried and failed and tried and failed and he didn't want to try again. He didn't want to let go of her. He didn't want to lose her. He'd lost enough.

But he knew how these things went.

He knew how these things ended.

"What do you want from me, Abaddon?" Luce's voice was low and menacing. He was done with this conversation.

Abaddon stepped forward, further into the street where Luce stood. "You know what I want. Join us, brother. Join me. Together we can take control and then nobody can tell us anything. Just imagine it, getting to make your own choices, not having to live by somebody else's rules."

"It's a nice dream, but that's all it is... a dream. I tried and failed."

"That's because you relied on force," Abaddon said. "You tried to physically take over, but we've got another plan, a different one that's almost guaranteed to work."

"What is it?"

"We're going to involve the humans."

Luce just stared at him. That wasn't a different plan. He'd tried that once with Eve.

"I know what you're thinking," Abaddon said. "You're thinking about what happened in the Garden of Eden, but it's a different world now. You seduced one human. I'm talking about six billion."

"And how exactly do you plan to pull that off?"

"We're going to show ourselves to them." Abaddon grinned. "To all of them."

Abaddon deliberately dropped his guard and let his thoughts flood through for Lucifer to observe. A hoard of angels, mostly Powers and Guardians, coming together to take over the earth. They were going to rise up and announce their existence. It all flashed through Luce's mind—public spectacles, with newspapers and television cameras, leading to bloodbaths and uprisings among the mortals, the death and destruction spanning the globe. The wave of devastation would move too fast, span too far, for their Father to clean it up with the wave of a hand. He'd conceal an angel's mess quickly to keep it from being discovered, but it was against his nature to intervene when it came to free will. The angels would capitalize on the chaos, and front and center in

Abaddon's plan was Lucifer.

Lucifer, the leader, standing in the middle of it all and watching as the world collapsed around him.

"Seems you have it all figured out," Luce said. "What do you need me for?"

"These humans, most of them don't know me... they don't know Hagith or Morael or Nanael, either. But you? They all know you. Lucifer is a name they learn in childhood. Satan... the proverbial devil... imagine their reaction if they knew he walked the earth. Imagine if they knew you mingled among them. I'm close to humans, so I know their hearts. Half of them don't even believe in God anymore, but they worry they may be wrong—not because they fear our Father but because they're terrified of *you*. They're afraid you exist. Imagine if they knew."

A thrilling tingle crept up Luce's spine. Exactly how many times during his stay in the pit had he dreamed of just that? It was everything he'd ever wanted... that was, until the day he wanted her.

In the short time since Serah had shown up at the gates, Luce's priorities had changed. He wasn't sure when it happened, or even why, but eventually his fight against the world turned into a fight for one soul, a soul that almost got damned for him. He'd never felt regret before... any angels that fell with him, or after him, had done it from their own choosing, had done it from their own actions, things they'd gotten into willingly. All of them, that is, except for Serah. He robbed her of her Grace, thrusting her into this other life, and now he was contemplating taking that world from her, too.

His tendency for selfishness, his penchant for greed, urged him to buy into his old friend's grand plan, but something else stopped him.

Something that felt infuriatingly like compassion.

Something that seemed to be a lot like loyalty.

Something like sympathy.

And empathy.

It was consideration.

Goddamned kindheartedness.

Who knew he had it in him?

"Thanks," Luce said, "but no thanks."

Abaddon's expression fell, his eyes darkening. That wasn't the answer he'd expected. Wasn't the response he'd wanted. "You're refusing?"

"I'm politely declining," Luce clarified as a surge of anger flowed through him. He could feel his fingertips tingling, desperate to purge it, the sky above them darkening with a sudden cloud covering as a gust of wind whipped between them. "It was a proposition, correct? An offer? You aren't so overconfident that you'd actually try to demand something of me, are you? Because I answer to nobody, Guardian... not you, not Michael, and not even Him."

"It was an offer," Abaddon said curtly. "One I don't understand why you won't take me up on."

"Because I won't be somebody's pawn," Luce said. "I've made that clear from the beginning of time. You can dress it up pretty, but I'm no fool. You want a face for your campaign, a scapegoat to accept the blame from above, and who better than the biggest villain of all, right? Who better than Satan to take the heat? But I'm done... I'm done fighting a lose battle for control of this shitty planet that I don't even want anymore. I wanted Paradise, but look around you, Don. Paradise is gone."

Abaddon's eyes narrowed. "I implore you to change your mind while you still can."

"While I *still* can? Is that a threat?"

"Just a suggestion," Abaddon said. "The world is changing, Lucifer, and soon. When the chips fall, you'll want yours to be on the winner, especially if you want *her* to stay safe."

Luce stepped toward him, going toe to toe, face to face. "And I have a suggestion for you."

"What?"

"Be careful what you say," Luce said. "You're full of empty promises, and one of these days, I might finally decide to hold you to them. When I do, you'll have a hell of a lot to atone for. So don't bury yourself too deep, or you might never fly off from the ground again."

"Ugh!" The groan seemed to echo through the yards. "Seriously?"

Serah glanced toward the house next door, toward the source of the voice, as she planted flowers in the patch of dirt beside her small porch. Next door, by the mailbox, the pregnant woman clutched her stomach as she tried to reach down to pick up some envelopes she'd dropped.

Serah was on her feet, heading right for her without a second thought. She quickly bent down and scooped up all the dropped mail, standing back up to hand it to her. "Here you go."

"Thank you so much," she said, taking the

envelopes. "You are Heaven-sent."

Serah smiled at that.

"I'm Samantha," the woman said. "You must be the new neighbor my daughter keeps going on about."

"Serah." She held her hand out, smiling as she used the name Luce had told her. It felt normal, like the name had given her a piece of her identity back. "Your daughter's a sweet child. She tried to help me when she thought I was lost."

"Yeah, that sounds like Nicki." Samantha shook her hand, smiling. "Would you like to come in for a drink or something?"

"Oh no, I wouldn't want to impose."

"You wouldn't be imposing."

"If you're certain..."

"I am," she said, matter-of-fact. "I would give just about anything for some adult conversation."

"Well, okay then," Serah said. "That sounds great."

As soon as Serah stepped inside the small house, a strange sensation tingled inside of her, setting her at ease. It was as if she'd been here before.

"Have a seat," Samantha said, motioning toward the small, round kitchen table. Serah slid into a chair as Samantha procured a bottle of wine from the fridge and two cups. It was nothing fancy—the cups were red disposable plastic, the wine straight off of a department store shelf, the price sticker still affixed to the bottle.

Samantha easily popped the cork, dumping quite a bit in one cup with just a splash in the other. She nudged the nearly full one toward Serah.

"I know, I know," Samantha said straight away. "Pregnant women aren't supposed to drink, and I don't... I haven't had a drop since I found out I was expecting. But after today, I need a sip... just a taste... *something*."

Serah smiled sadly. "Bad day?"

"That's an understatement," she said, dropping down onto the chair right across from Serah. Up close, the woman looked exhausted, but a warm smile graced her lips anyway. "I'm so tired, I can't sleep, don't even have enough energy to keep up with Nicki, and my husband called this morning to say they're switching to twelve-hour shifts. Which is great, you know, because we need the money, but I'd love to have my husband around more."

"I'm sure he'd love to be around more, too," Serah said, the words flowing from her lips without a thought as she picked up the cup and sniffed it. It smelled like sour grapes. She'd never drunk wine before.

"Yeah, I know he would," Samantha agreed, throwing back her swallow. Closing her eyes and tilting her head back, she swished the wine around in her mouth for a moment before spitting it right back into the cup. She smiled sheepishly before pushing the cup aside and continuing. "Nicholas—my husband—works hard, and as much as I appreciate everything he does, all I seem to feel these days is what he can't do. Parenting, housework, yard work... I'll be wading through knee-high grass before long on my journey to get the stack of bills from the mailbox. Waddling as I go, of course, thanks to this one."

Samantha rubbed her stomach over her shirt.

"How far along are you?" Serah asked curiously.

"Eight months," she said. "He's due in four weeks."

"He?"

"Yep, a boy," she said. "Samuel."

The sound of that name hit Serah like a ton of bricks. Her insides felt like they were on fire, warmth spreading through her. "Samuel," she whispered. She couldn't quite place it, but that name felt as familiar as her own had the first time she heard it.

"He was a surprise," Samantha continued. "We weren't going to have any more after Nicki, but I guess God had other plans for us. Anyway, listen to me going on and on. Tell me about yourself, neighbor."

Serah was quiet for a moment, staring down into the cup at the liquid, a deep crimson color. "I'm afraid there's not much to tell."

Serah recounted what she could, giving a summarized version of herself. A few brief sentences to sum up a forgotten lifetime.

"Wow, that's... wow." Samantha stared at her, dumbfounded. "You remember nothing from before the big storm?"

"Nothing," Serah replied, but a tingle inside of her told her she was telling a lie. Images flashed in her mind, the same images that had assaulted her when Luce kissed her in her living room. It had been just a few days ago, his absence afterward a hard pill to swallow. He'd vanished and hadn't resurfaced.

She was still questioning her sanity.

"You poor thing." Samantha reached over, grasping Serah's hand, the contact sending a buzz through her that made her heart race. It was like being zapped in the chest. "I can't imagine what it must be like."

Before Serah could respond, a screech echoed

from a back bedroom, little footsteps running down the hallway. Serah glanced up as Nicki ran into the kitchen, clutching a notebook. The little girl was rambling something about a drawing but froze, eyes widening when she saw Serah sitting there.

"Hey!" she said excitedly, skirting right past her mother to run for Serah instead. "I just drew you!"

Serah tensed as Samantha let out a laugh. Nicki leaped up in the chair right beside Serah, slamming her notebook down on the table in front of them. Serah glanced at the picture, joining Samantha in laughter at what she saw: a woman, in a long tan colored dress, holding a green blob in her hands.

"It's a frog," Nicki exclaimed, pointing at it. "Did you find yours yet?"

"I don't know that I have," Serah said hesitantly.

"Too bad." Nicki said it casually, shrugging. "Maybe you will today."

The little girl was off again, running for the door as she shouted back at her mother that she was going outside to play. Samantha yelled to her, telling her to tie her shoes, asking her to be careful, shouting to her about safety, but Nicki was out the door without listening to a bit of it. Groaning, Samantha shoved her chair back and climbed to her feet. "I wish I had half of her energy."

"Luckily, I do," Serah said, jumping to her feet. "Allow me."

Samantha looked as if she wanted to argue but shrugged it off, slumping back into the chair. Serah headed outside, finding Nicki in the front yard, the grass nearly to her small waist. Serah helped the girl tie her shoes and relayed the messages from her mother before heading back inside. She retook the seat at the table, picking up the yet untouched glass of wine, as Samantha eyed her peculiarly.

"Did she put up a fight?"

"No."

"She listened to you?"

"Yes."

A smile overtook Samantha's lips. "Serah, I think you and I are going to be great friends."

Serah let out a light laugh as she brought the cup to her lips, hesitantly taking a small sip of the wine. It was bitter, and kind of warm, but it went down smoothly. Serah pulled the cup back, glancing inside of it, before taking another sip right away.

Three sips later, her body was tingly.

Another four and she felt like she was floating above the chair.

The two chatted as they sat at the kitchen table,

late afternoon turning into early evening. Serah drank the wine and happily listened while Samantha vented her frustrations. By the time night fell outside, Nicki was sitting with them, coloring contentedly. Both women were relaxed, a weight seemed to have lifted off of Samantha's shoulders, while Serah was downright buzzing.

All mortals have sin inside of them.

In some, it's barely measurable, little drops of depravity that never floated to the surface, staying buried deep inside the body. Others wear their sins like tattoos on the skin, badges they carelessly flash at anyone who comes near.

Luce had encountered them all—the selfish mostly full of greed, the lazy filled to the brim with sloth, the evil fed by wrath, the jealous consumed by envy, the conceited with their inflated pride, and the gluttons with their overindulging—but he'd always been drawn to the ones bathed in lust. Pheromones coated them like an intoxicating perfume. In the past, he rarely resisted the scent. He drowned himself in it, sometimes not coming up for air for days… weeks… months.

Years.

He'd walk away from a binge of sin, coated in all of the deadliest, his eyes blazing embers, his skin pulsating. In the aftermath, he'd feel like that indestructible being, the villainous monster the world made him out to be. He wouldn't think twice about those he destroyed during his rampage, the souls he'd shredded, the torture he'd inflicted.

He was a junkie, plain and simple...

And he hadn't had a taste in months.

Luce stood in front of Serah's house. The lights were all off inside, nobody home, but he could sense her essence strongly next door. It was a powerful concentration, humming like a motor, the vibration so intense Luce could feel the ground trembling beneath his feet. Her energy still buzzed on a higher frequency than everyone else, and tonight, it was loud.

It practically screamed.

He'd been half a world away, on another continent, in the ancient castle where the demons still flocked, passing his time sitting in that throne and tinkering with his knife. He'd sent his minions out to keep an eye on Abaddon, and they reported back every few hours with what he was doing.

Nothing.

He was doing fucking nothing.

Luce wasn't an idiot, though. The angel was biding his time before he enacted his plan. Luce was waiting for his old friend to set things in motion, but he didn't want the fight to be drawn anywhere near her.

So he kept his distance, but it didn't last long, because he felt the pull from over three thousand miles away. He'd zapped right there, unable to ignore it, and the concentration of sin nearly knocked him on his ass.

Lust.

Small doses had brewed in her as an angel. He'd felt them then. He'd capitalized on them. But this? This was like nothing he'd ever felt from her before.

Luce stood still, watching as Serah exited the neighbor's house and strolled through the yard toward hers. She was light on her feet, but somewhat unsteady, weaving as she strolled along. She glanced up when she neared her porch, gasping and stopping abruptly. "Luce."

His name was a whisper. Her breath smelled like wine. Her cheeks flushed pink from her intoxication, and the wave of desire struck him hard. His own body started buzzing from it, a needless breath entering his lungs as he inhaled the aroma. He needn't see himself

173

to know his eyes were dimming, the purity draining from him. He could feel it, feel the flames igniting under his skin, his temperature steadily rising.

Sinners run hot because they're destined to burn.

It's Hell's way of calling them home.

"Serah," he said quietly, his voice strained as he addressed her.

"Luce," she said again. "I haven't seen you."

"I haven't been around."

It was the longest Luce had stayed away from her in months.

"I know. You left."

"I did."

"But you're here," she said, stepping toward him. "You're here now."

"I am."

She stared up at him, her breaths shaky. He could see she had a dozen other questions, her mouth opening and closing as she struggled to form them. She remained silent, though. The words wouldn't come out.

Carefully, Luce reached over, grazing his fingertips along her flushed cheek, feeling the warmth brewing beneath her skin. Touching her was dangerous. His fix was right in front of him, glowing like a beacon, calling out to him. He could satiate his need and purge the build up, drawing the lust out of her as she welcomed him in. And she would. She yearned for him. He could feel it stronger at that moment than he ever felt it down in the pit.

Luce started to speak but the words were stolen from him when Serah thrust up on her tiptoes, lips smashing against his. The moment they connected, all thoughts wiped from his mind as he blanked out, feeling nothing, seeing nothing, except for her.

Energy surged inside of him. Snatching a hold of Serah, he dragged her inside, never breaking the kiss. He pulled her through the house, frustration mingling with the powerful sensation. It was so damn difficult not being able to zap her anywhere.

He found the bedroom and easily lifted her up by her hips, pulling her onto the small bed, on top of the crisp, cool sheets. Her dress bunched up around her hips as he settled between her legs, kissing her deeply, tasting the wine on her lips.

His hands roamed her body, caressing her skin, groping her flesh. He thrust against her, material still separating them, but the friction was enough to push Serah over the edge. She moaned into his mouth, her sighs becoming cries that Luce feasted on, hungrily devouring every whimper as he thrust, and thrust, and thrust. He nearly knocked her off the bed from the force, the headboard banging against the wall as he fucked her with their clothes on, not once breaking the kiss.

It was enough... just enough... for him to get a taste, to give her what she yearned for, but it wasn't what Luce really craved. He wanted her. All of her. Lust wasn't enough. He wanted to pull everything out of her and bask in it.

He thrust harder, and harder, feeling her body quiver beneath his as she started to come. She called out to him, the shaky cry of pleasure exiting her and flowing through him. His body lit up from the inside, tingling from head to toe, as a sudden and unexpected crash of thunder rumbled, lightning flashing right outside the window.

He tilted his head back, absorbing it all.

"Oh God," Serah whimpered. Luce's hand clamped down around her mouth, smothering the words. Her eyes shot open, startled, as he looked at her.

"Be careful who you invoke," he said quietly, his body rubbing against hers, riding her through the orgasm, as he stared her in the eyes. He could see a reflection of his own--pitch black. At least they weren't red. Red would terrify her, but right now she just looked intrigued.

He pulled his hand away just as her voice rang out. "Your eyes are so dark... and your skin is burning up. I feel like... I feel like I'm humming. Like my soul is vibrating because of your touch."

It is, Lucifer thought. He recharged her energy just by getting her off. Lust still clung to her, surrounding both of them, but he'd siphoned most of it off.

Without responding, his hands cupped her face. He kissed her again, kissing her deeply, as her body started to relax into the bed.

"You're sleeping," he whispered against her lips. "You're dreaming, angel. This didn't happen."

Pulling back, he hovered over of her and stared down into her eyes. She held his gaze for a moment as he brushed his fingertips across her forehead.

Her eyes fluttered closed.

Out cold for the night.

Tension smothered the throne room.

Michael had never felt such suffocation before,

his chest tight like his lungs needed air but he couldn't breath. He clutched the hilt of his sword tightly with both hands, the tip of it grinding into the floor.

He couldn't move, or speak. He couldn't do anything. He was made of marble. He'd been chiseled from stone.

Inside, he felt like he was crumbling.

"I warned you," his Father said gently.

Michael lowered his head and closed his eyes. "I know."

The throne room had been broadcasting images of Satan for months. It played out around them like a long, endless movie, day in and day out. The same settings, the same cast. Michael avoided most of it, but curiosity got the best of him today. Serah had succumbed to mortal temptations, and Satan had been drawn right to it.

Of course. Even Michael had felt the attraction, the pull of sin from so far away. Serah wasn't used to human emotions. When the switch flipped inside of her, it was extreme.

Michael stayed planted in Heaven, though, and despite his Father's warnings, he watched it play out. Michael wanted to bear witness to the evil, but what he'd seen was an entirely different show. Satan had purged it from her, reveling in the sin himself, but he'd left her intact afterward.

He didn't further taint her soul.

"Is it because she's mortal now?" Michael asked quietly. "Is that why she responds to him so?"

In all the time they'd been together, Michael had never seen Serah so unguarded, so passionate. He'd never heard such cries of pleasure.

"Partly," He responded. "It's the combination of them together, son. Lucifer is sulfuric acid, sometimes dangerous but still valuable. Serah, on the other hand, is water, peaceful and pure. Mixed together, those two are fine, as long as you introduce the acid slowly. The other way around, you're headed for destruction. Dump water straight into the acid and something may very well explode."

Made sense, on the surface, but Michael had difficulties accepting it.

Why them? Why not him?

Why? Why? Why?

"You know why," He said, easily tapping into Michael's thoughts. "It was destined."

"For how long?"

Was it always supposed to be this way? The

entire time he'd been with Serah, had He known it would happen? Had He planned this?

"It was written in the stars the day Lucifer fell," He said. "She was destined to save him from himself."

"Has she?" Michael asked. "Has he been saved?"

His Father cocked his head to the side, staring at the projection of Lucifer. He stood just outside Serah's house again as she slept soundly in bed. "I'm not sure."

The hesitance in his Father's voice bewildered Michael. That was the second time He had wavered, the second time He seemed to not know. "How can you not be sure? You know all. You see all."

"I do."

"Then you must see his future."

"I do," He said. "But Lucifer possesses something unpredictable."

"What?"

"Free will."

Michael was stunned. *Free will?*

"He's one of a kind," He said. "He walks free, controlling his own destiny, but he doesn't yet know himself. His mind isn't made up. It changes every few seconds, altering the future in vastly different ways."

Michael turned from his Father. "Why can't I see it?" He strained, trying to sense the future like he did with mortals, but there was nothing. He shifted, trying to sense Serah's, but hers, too, was blank. "I can't see her, either."

"I've kept them from you," He said.

Why? Michael wondered, but his Father didn't answer his question. Not this time. They watched the image of Satan for a moment longer before the fallen angel zapped away. His Father waved his hand, the picture dissolving.

"If she doesn't save him?" Michael asked. "What if he makes the wrong decision?"

"Then everyone will lose," He responded. "Especially them."

It was the middle of the afternoon on a Tuesday. Samantha Lauer sat at her kitchen table, feet propped up in the chair beside her, barefoot and wearing a pair of raggedy pajamas. Her ankles were swollen, her back was aching, and she'd give her left tit for the heartburn to go away.

Serah knew all of this because she sat right across

from her new friend, listening as she vented. The end of summer was upon them. They'd spent the past few weeks getting to know one another, hanging out in the afternoon before Serah headed off to work the night shift at the motel.

The windows were wide open, a warm breeze wafting through the room. Sweat accumulated on Serah's brow, beading along her nape and running down her back.

"Ugh, this boy," Samantha groaned, clutching her stomach as she stood up. "You'd think I was giving birth to Charlie Watts with the way he drums on my bladder all day long."

Serah laughed, finishing off the rest of her glass of lemonade as Samantha wandered down the hall to the bathroom for the fifth time in an hour. Serah stood up, taking her empty cup to the sink, when the front door of the house opened. She glanced over as Samantha's husband, Nicholas, stepped inside. He started to speak but silenced when he glanced over and saw it wasn't his wife standing there.

"Oh, hey," he said, nodding politely.

Serah smiled. "Hello."

She didn't have much contact with Nicholas, meeting him a few times in passing when he was home, but he seemed like a good man.

"Where's Sam?" he asked, raising an eyebrow, a twinge of worry in his voice. "Is she—?"

"Relax," Samantha called out, making her way back to the kitchen. "I'm right here. What are you doing home?"

"Thought I'd check on you," he said, "so I came home for lunch."

Samantha kissed her husband before shuffling to the fridge. "I'm fine. Now sit down and I'll make you something."

Serah took that as her cue to leave, ignoring their declarations that she should stay and at least have a sandwich. She made her way through the tall grass to her home and headed into the bathroom, stripping out of her clothes to take a cold shower.

Climbing under the spray, she stood there, letting the water rain down on her, cooling her clammy skin. Her eyes drifted closed but flashed back open within seconds when a banging echoed through the house.

Somebody was knocking on the door.

Sighing, Serah turned off the water, cutting her shower short as the banging echoed through the house once more. Stepping out, she grabbed a towel and wrapped it around herself, opening the bathroom door. The moment she did, she nearly ran right into someone. Gasping, grabbing her chest, she nearly lost the towel as she recoiled.

Luce.

He was inside her house, standing in the hallway right outside the bathroom door. "Jesus!"

"No, it's me," he said. "Jesus isn't around."

Serah rolled her eyes, clutching the towel closed. "Was that you?"

"Was what me?"

"The banging."

He needn't answer, as the sound rang out once more. Serah's eyes darted past Luce, settling on the door, her brow furrowing. Clearly it hadn't been him. She had half a dozen questions, like where'd he come from, where had he been, and how in the world had he ended up in her house, but the frantic knocking distracted her.

"No," Luce said, casting a glance at the door. "Not me."

Serah pushed past him, heading for the door, and carefully tugged it open. Nicholas stood on the other side, eyes panicked.

"Nicholas? What's wrong?"

"I hate to do this... I hate to ask you this. I know

we hardly know each other, but my wife really likes you, and my daughter does, too. So I'm just wondering if you could do me a favor, if there's any way you can watch Nicki this afternoon for us?"

"Uh, sure," Serah said. "No problem."

"She's at day camp. The bus will drop her off in about an hour. If you could just watch her for a bit, we'd be eternally grateful."

"Absolutely."

"We can pay you," he continued.

"Nonsense," she said. "It'll be my pleasure."

"Thank you." Relief tinged his voice. "Truly, thank you."

"Of course."

Nicholas started to rush away when Serah called out to him.

"Wait," she said. "Is something happening?"

He glanced back at her, his expression lighting up, swallowing back the fear. "Sam's water just broke. We're having a baby!"

A smile graced Serah's lips as she watched Nicholas sprint next door. She stood in the doorway, just staring out at the street, until the voice behind her startled her from her daze. "It's a little indecent, don't you think?"

She turned, eyeing Luce from a few feet away. "What?"

"You," he said. "Wearing that, right here, right now."

Glancing down, Serah felt her cheeks flushing as she quickly closed the front door. "Where did you even come from?"

"Loaded question."

"How did you get here?"

"I'm not certain you want to know."

She eyed him hesitantly as he evaded answering her questions. "I don't recall inviting you inside."

"Oh, but you did," he said. "Weeks ago."

"That doesn't count."

"Why not?"

"Because that was then and this is now."

Luce just stared at her. Serah could feel her blush deepening further at his intense gaze and fidgeted a bit, clutching hold of the towel around her to keep herself concealed. She feigned annoyance at his company, pretending to be put off by his presence, but truthfully she felt at ease about him being in her home. She'd just been surprised, not at all disturbed.

She should've been, though.

It should've bothered her. Frightened her.

There was nothing normal about the situation, nothing safe about these circumstances, but she couldn't seem to force herself to be troubled.

It felt natural, like he'd been there all along.

"Do you want me to go?" Luce asked as she strolled toward him.

"No," she whispered, stepping around him. "I don't."

Lucifer stared hard at the tattered cards in his hand. The edges of them were singed and the white was tinted a grimy shade of gray. They'd seen a lot of play over time, and he was definitely due for a new deck, but he had an attachment to these.

They were the ones Serah played with him down in the pit.

The deck had been through thousands of games of War, had seen hundreds of rounds of Solitaire, but none had been as strenuous as the battle it saw now.

"Does you have sixes?"

Lucifer's eyes stayed fixed to his hand. "*Does* I have sixes," he repeated, muttering the grammatically fucked up words under his breath.

"Yes." Her voice was serious... so, so serious. "Does you?"

Luce stared at the two sixes in his hand for a second before his gaze shifted overtop his cards, meeting a pair of wide, brown eyes. Nicki Barlow. The little girl stared him down, waiting about as patiently as a nine-year-old could wait.

Go fish. Those words were on the tip of his tongue. Anyone else, and he would've said them. Anyone else, and he would've lied. But she looked at him with the same sort of reverence that Lucifer once felt toward his Father. She trusted him implicitly to tell the truth.

Grudgingly, Luce pulled out the two sixes and handed them over. Squealing excitedly, Nicki formed a book, putting all of the sixes in front of her. She was winning now, two to one.

"Does you have any queens?" she asked, going again.

Luce didn't have to look at his hand. "Go fish."

Nicki drew a card from the pile.

"Give me your kings," Luce said.

Nicki didn't even think before saying, "Go fish."

Luce pulled a card from the pile and was arranging it in his hand when she spoke. "Does you have kings?"

Luce froze, no part of him moving except his eyes as they darted to her. "What did you just ask for?"

"Kings."

"That's what I asked you for," he said, tone clipped as he glared at the girl. "You said you didn't have any."

She shook her head, steadfast. "Nuh-uh. I do have them. See?"

She held up a king to show him.

It took everything inside of Luce not to snatch it from her hand.

Un-fucking-believable. He detected nothing but innocence inside of her, no sort of benevolence beneath her skin, even though she'd just lied right to his face. He hadn't had a creature baffle him so much since Serah. Children, to him, were an unknown entity. Children didn't go to the pit.

This tiny mortal felt no shame for manipulating him, had no remorse for lying to win the game.

That was his M.O.

He had to admit, he was impressed. Carefully, he pulled the kings from his hand and wordlessly passed them over to her, letting her, for the moment, get away with cheating him.

The game went on for a few more minutes before

Serah stepped into her living room where they sat, Luce on the couch and Nicki cross-legged on the floor on the opposite side of the coffee table.

"Who's winning?" Serah asked casually.

"Me!" Nicki exclaimed.

Walking over, Serah plopped down on the couch beside Luce, sitting so close her body brushed against his. She leaned over, resting her head on his shoulder as she glanced at the cards in his hand. Luce tensed at the contact, largely trying to ignore it to focus on the game. Her touch felt stronger with his shield down, making himself visible.

The things he did for her...

"Does you have fours?" Nicki asked.

Luce turned a four over to her, although he was pretty damn sure he had asked her for those not long ago. She asked for another king next and drew a card to go fish, as Luce cleared his throat. "Give me your twos."

As soon as the words were from his lips, Serah elbowed him in the side. "Geez, you can't ask?"

Luce cut his eyes at her. "What?"

"Give me your twos." She mocked him, the words low and gritty as she tried to emulate his voice. "You sound so demanding... so mean."

Mean?

If only she knew who she was talking to...

"Fine," Luce said. "Do you have any twos?"

"Go Fish!"

The game went on for a few more rounds before Luce gathered enough matches to pull ahead. They were two books away from completion when Nicki suddenly jumped to her feet, throwing the rest of her cards down. "I'm done playing now."

Luce gaped at her. "You can't be *done.*"

"Why?"

"Because I was about to win."

Nicki shrugged, turning her attention to Serah. "Can I go outside and play? Please?"

Serah hesitated before smiling. "Sure, just stay where I can see you."

Luce stared at the little girl as she skipped away, disappearing out the front door. She'd been there for less than an hour and Luce was already frazzled because of her. His gaze shifted to the discarded cards. No one had ever just quit on him before.

Mostly because they couldn't, he wouldn't allow it, but still...

Reaching over, Luce gathered all the cards from the table and started shuffling them. He shifted his body slightly, turning toward Serah beside him. She was staring straight ahead, watching out the large window at Nicki running around the front yard.

As if she could see his gaze, a small smile lifted her lips, her cheeks flushing slightly. "So strange," she whispered.

Luce certainly agreed with that. "Children are strange creatures."

She turned his way. "I was referring to you."

"Ah, I'm not so strange," he said. "I'm not much different than you."

"People think I'm strange," she counters.

"Do they tell you that?" Luce asked curiously, defensiveness prickling inside of him. He knew humans could be cruel. He wasn't always around to hear what they said to her.

"No, but I know they do," she said quietly. "I can sense it."

Her answer surprised Luce.

"I know what you're thinking," she said right away, continuing. "That I'm crazy, thinking I can sense it, but I do. I sense a lot, and maybe it's all in my head... I don't know. But I get feelings about things that I can't shake."

"What kind of feelings?"

She sighed. "All kinds. I know things, things I shouldn't know. I can tell when someone's being genuine or when they're just humoring me. I can walk into a crowded room and automatically be drawn to someone, one person among dozens, and I just get this overwhelming urge to talk to them. I walk down the street and find myself somewhere I hadn't planned to go, like some force lured me there. It's like I have some kind of radar."

"Maybe you do," Luce said, "but it's not fool-proof."

"And how do you know?"

"Because that wasn't what I was thinking. I don't think you're crazy, Serah. I think you're special."

"Like you," she said. "You said we weren't much different, after all."

He smiled at that. Special? There was no denying it. He was special. He'd been purposely created that way. The debate had always been whether or not it was for the good.

"We are alike," he said, continuing to shuffle. "The difference being I wish I could forget everything you no longer remember."

"And I wish I could remember."

"I know you do."

J.M. Darhower

"I wish you'd tell me."

"And I wish I could."

She was quiet for a moment, just watching him shuffle. "I sensed things about you, too, you know."

"I'd be surprised if you hadn't."

Her eyes narrowed contemplatively as she stared at his hands before meeting his gaze. "You're a stranger to me, Luce. In my head, I don't really know anything about you. You walk around barefoot, you find shoes out of nowhere, you order an apple for breakfast but you don't eat it, and you're always there. Everywhere I look, you're there, and then you're gone again. It's not normal."

Normal is relative, he wanted to say. Fuck normal anyway.

Before he could say anything, though, she continued.

"You're a stranger to me," she said again, "but somehow I know you. I see you pop up out of nowhere, I find you standing in my hallway, or lurking outside of my work, and my heart starts to race, but it isn't because I'm afraid. It races, because it knows you. It skips a beat, because it knows you're there. My heart knows you even though the rest of me doesn't."

194

Luce's eyes drifted down toward her chest briefly before looking at the cards in his hand. Her heart was beating steadily, melodically. "It's not racing now. It's been at ease today."

"You can tell that?"

He shrugged a shoulder, absently dividing the deck of cards down the middle and pushing half of it toward her. "You want to play?"

Carefully, she picked up the partial deck. "What are we playing?"

"War."

"War," she repeated, starting to turn her cards over, but Luce reached over, grasping her hand, stopping her before she looked at them. He quickly ran through the basics of the game as she stared down at his hand on top of hers. When he was finished, she looked back up at him. "I've played this before."

She posed it as a statement, but Luce could see the questions in her eyes. "Yeah, you have."

"Did I play it with you?"

"Many times."

"Did I win?"

"Once."

She nodded, shifting to face him more as she smiled. "Well, Luce, it's about to be twice."

He laughed, amused, as they started playing. Twenty minutes later, Serah won the game.

"We really appreciate this," Nicholas whispered, standing on the front porch, a sleeping Nicki wrapped around him, drooling on his shoulder. "Seriously, I can't thank you enough."

"I told you it was my pleasure," Serah said. "If you need anything else, I'm here."

Nicholas smiled. "You might live to regret that."

Serah laughed. "Never."

Nicholas departed after thanking her a few more times. Serah waited until they were out of sight before closing the front door and leaning back against it. It was nearing three o'clock in the morning and Serah had missed work. Her boss had understood, but it still weighed heavily on her.

Serah's gaze shifted around the room in the darkness, the only source of light from a very dim lamp. Luce sat still right in the center of the couch, elbows resting on his knees, eyes on her. He'd stayed the entire evening, never once complaining that he had somewhere else to be.

Did he? She couldn't help but wonder. *Where did he go when he had to leave?*

As if on cue, he rose to his feet. "I should go."

"Stay."

The single word from her lips stalled him. He stood there, still staring at her in the darkness, as he seemed to contemplate it. After a moment, he stepped toward her, cradling her face between his hands. His thumbs lightly stroked her cheeks.

"You're beautiful, angel," he whispered. "You sure you want me to stay?"

She nodded.

She wasn't sure the implication of it, what his staying truly meant, but the thought of him leaving made her chest tight. Parts of her ached, aching to be reacquainted with what she used to know, with what she used to be with him. It was the closest to remembering she got. She wanted that.

Maybe she wanted *him*.

Leaning down, he softly kissed her, the lightest touch of their lips. Without deepening it, he picked her up, and Serah gasped in his mouth as he carried her through the house. He took her right back to the only bedroom, laying her on the center of the bed.

Serah relaxed as Luce's lips left hers to instead

explore her skin. He kissed her face, her jawline, her neck, sending tingles deep down through her body as he kissed her again and again.

His hands roamed, gently caressing her. He tugged her dress up over her head when she raised her hands, letting him take it off. His lips traveled the length of her torso, easily shedding the rest of her clothes.

His mouth found the apex of her thighs. Sparks ignited inside of her as she arched her back, her hands in his hair. It was soft, much softer than she expected from someone constructed from such harsh lines and dark features. He kissed her, tasted her, caressing her flesh with his tongue.

Pleasure tore through her, orgasm gripping her as her muscles twitched. She cried out, and he didn't let up, continuing the motions until the sensations subsided and she relaxed again.

She lay there, breathing heavily, body tingling, as he tore off his own clothes haphazardly. Her eyes trailed over his naked form, mesmerized by the lines and contours. He was stunning, absolutely perfect, no flaws or blemishes, nothing out of place. Even the mark that had not long ago been carved in his chest was gone, fully healed, having faded away.

Luce stared down at her, something brewing in his eyes, unexpectedly dark. Her back prickled with a sense of danger, but desire shoved it aside.

Maybe he was dangerous, but for some reason, she trusted him.

"So beautiful," he said again, voice rough and gritty as his hands massaged her breasts. "You sure about this?"

All it took was another nod.

She didn't even have to speak.

Luce settled between her thighs, meeting her lips again as he pushed inside of her. Serah moaned as he filled her, an overwhelming sensation swarming her. She felt warm, so warm, like he was kindling a fire in her bones. He moved slowly at first, letting her adjust to the feeling, before increasing the pace just a bit.

Breaking the kiss, he pulled back, his hand coming to rest on her chest, on top of the circular scar over her heart. His palm felt like burning embers, searing flames, as her heart frantically pounded against it.

"It's racing now," he whispered. "I can hear it."

He made love to her, thrusting again and again, propping himself up with one arm as his right hand stayed planted on her chest. Serah didn't just feel him in body. Luce was penetrating part of her soul. He wrapped himself tightly around it, gripping hold and not letting go, claiming parts of Serah she didn't realize existed until he awakened them in her. Outside, thunder rumbled in the distance, wind whipping against the windows as a storm neared.

Another orgasm seized her, and then another, back to back pleasure sending her over the edge. She could barely catch her breath as he drove her places she wasn't sure a human body was capable of being. His name fell from her lips, a gratifying whisper she couldn't contain.

Luce.

"So beautiful," he whispered yet again, his mouth finding her ear as she closed her eyes, wrapping her arms tightly around him, holding him even though it hurt. Stinging erupted across her skin, torturous pins and needles that left a burn in their wake. It felt like sunburn, rubbed raw, making tears prickle the corner of her eyes.

He moved faster, thrusting deeper, muttering into her neck about being close. Serah could sense it, could feel his body tensing, rock hard above her, his movements more frenzied. The ache inside of her intensified as she squeezed her eyes shut tightly, a tear leaking down her cheek.

"No," Luce growled. "No... no... no..."

All at once, the blackness ripped away with a blast of light, burning blood red behind her eyelids as another orgasm ripped through her. She gasped, struggling for air. It was as if an explosion went off inside of her chest, ricocheting out through her limbs. Her eyes snapped open, and maybe it was her imagination, but she could've sworn he was glowing again.

"NO!"

Lucifer screamed the word as the stark white spans of nothingness materialized around him, his bare feet planted dead center of the circle surrounded by those damned confining sigils. He glared down at them, anger building inside of him, brewing like molten lava.

He felt like he might explode.

He could feel the peculiar tingle from being summoned, but the rage overshadowed it, the concentration of sin inside of him so intense it made his body vibrate. He clenched his hands into fists, trying to restrain it, to force it back, but it had been building for too long.

It had nowhere to go.

"Fuck!"

The curse roared from his lips, the feelings purging from him at once. It had been so long, too long, since he opened up and just let it go, unleashing everything that he'd been bottling in. The release of energy was so intense the floor quaked, for just a moment everything surrounding him obscured in a haze, like the brightness of Heaven had been soiled by all of his sin. It cleared just as quickly as it happened, the ground stable as it was all sucked away.

Lucifer's fiery gaze lifted from the sigils surrounding him, imprisoning him, to the throne just a few feet away. His Father sat passively, relaxed, merely watching him with a bored expression on His face. Michael, on the other hand, sat hunched over, slumped with defeat, his face lined with concern and a tinge of something else.

Disgust?

"Are you done now?" His father asked calmly, "or do you want to throw another tantrum?"

Tantrum. Luce hated being spoken to like a child.

Luce didn't entertain that condescending question with an answer, keeping his eyes on Michael. No, it wasn't disgust, nor was it anger. It was hurt.

Hurt.

How many times had he tried to hurt his brother? How many times had he tried to destroy Michael only to decide, at the end, the archangel couldn't be wounded? Clearly, he'd been wrong.

He'd hurt him finally.

Luce didn't feel quite so good about it today.

He knew, taking in Michael's expression, that he'd witnessed what just happened, that he'd seen every bit of his evening with Serah. What kind of sick, masochistic voyeur would watch that?

"Lucifer."

His Father's voice was strong, an edge of authority to it that instinctively drew his eyes to Him. Luce suddenly felt extremely exposed, standing in the middle of Heaven in front of his dysfunctional family wearing nothing but Serah's scent and a hell of a lot of sin, his mind an open book.

Lucifer tried to manifest some clothes, but the enchantments around him kept him from doing much of anything. Groaning, he glared at his Father. "Give me some clothes."

"Clothes?" He asked casually. "You've never been one for modesty. You seem to get a lot of pleasure out of the naked form."

"Yeah, well, I'm not entirely getting pleasure out of having my brother over there ogle my cock."

Michael chimed in, disgruntled. "I would never!"

Their Father raised His hand, silencing Michael before he could truly argue. With the flick of a wrist, clothes materialized on Luce, the same clothes he'd been granted so many years ago, clothes that matched Michael's—a crisp, clean suit, so white it blended into their surroundings.

Luce cocked an eyebrow at the getup. "Really?"

His Father simply smiled.

"Put me back," Luce ordered. "You had no business calling me here, no business watching me, no business intervening in what we were doing. She has free will. There's nothing to stop her from being with me if she wants to be. So put me back. *Now.*"

Luce's demands went ignored.

"Do you know why angels are forbidden from intermingling with humans?" his Father asked.

"Because You're an asshole?"

"Because you're powerful," He said, ignoring the insult as usual. "You especially, Lucifer. You're the most powerful being I ever created. With the exception of your brother, few creatures could ever cause the sort of chaos that you do. And while he's capable of the same level of destruction, he doesn't have it in him to ever do it. Not like you."

Those words were constricting, like hands wrapped around Lucifer's throat. "Guess they're wrong, huh? Your beloved children think God doesn't make mistakes."

"I don't," He said firmly. "You're not a mistake."

"What am I then? An experiment gone awry? Some kind of fucking plaything for you to toy with?"

"You're you," He said, as if that cleared it up. "You're my child, Lucifer."

Luce just stared at Him. He had a steadfast argument against that, but he didn't have it in him to get into it again.

"Put me back."

"You're too strong for her."

"I'll hold back."

"You can't."

"Don't tell me what to do!" Lucifer snapped. "I take orders from no one!"

All was quiet for a moment, tension building then releasing from the room as his Father sent a wave of calm through the air that only scarcely affected Luce.

"No one underestimates you as much as you do yourself," He said. "Your power once wiped out most of her Grace. Even restrained, you siphoned off so much of her innocence. She was an angel then, strong, but she was no match for you, and she's mortal now. She's weak. You're lethal to her."

"I'll be careful."

"You nearly exploded her heart," He said quietly. "Had I not pulled you away when I did, your power would've taken her life. It would've drained her until she had nothing left."

Luce didn't want to believe it.

It hurt him to even entertain it.

"I'll put you back," He continued. "If that's what you truly want."

Luce nodded. "I certainly don't want to be *here*."

With the snap of a finger, everything was gone, the darkness of Serah's bedroom surrounding him once again. He was deep inside of her, so deep he could feel the fire in her, could feel her frantic heartbeat as it pulsated through him. Orgasm rocked through her, so hard her heart stalled for a moment and fell out of rhythm.

Her eyes shot open, meeting his, the irises burning bright red. Fuck. Luce pulled out of her instantly before he went too far, easing his grip on her skin. He'd been close. So fucking close. He'd been so lost in the sensations he hadn't sensed her oncoming distress. She stared up at him in shock, blinking rapidly after a second. "What was that?"

The earth still trembled around him, the storm outside beating down on them now. It had been him, he realized. The purge of emotions had caused it. He'd been gone for only a fraction of a second, not long enough for Serah to detect, but she certainly felt the after affects.

"It's just a storm," he said. "Lightning and thunder."

Serah's heart rate eased just a bit, her eyes softening to their usual brown, a slight glow lingering on her skin. He leaned down, softly kissing her, just a gentle peck before he brought his lips to her forehead.

"Get some sleep," he whispered, more to himself than her, because she was unconscious within seconds. "You're going to need to recuperate."

Four

Samantha Lauer still couldn't sleep.

It wasn't the heartburn or the swollen ankles that did it. She had something more invasive now: a crying infant.

He was a tiny thing, the smallest person Serah had ever seen, but he wailed loudly. He fit perfectly in the crook of his mother's arm, nearly invisible if it weren't for the ear-splitting screech. Serah sat across from them at the kitchen table, her eyes on the little round face.

Even distraught, she'd never seen something so lovely.

It amazed her, something coming from nothing, developing and evolving from the tiniest cells, the universe breathing life into a woman's body. She'd never thought of having children, or at least she didn't remember ever thinking of it, but seeing little Samuel in his mother's arms made a part of Serah twinge.

"He's beautiful, Samantha."

"He's unhappy," Samantha said. "He hates me."

Her distressed voice made Serah smile sympathetically. "No, he doesn't. Children don't hate their parents."

"You sure about that?"

"Positive," she said. "He's just trying to communicate."

"Yeah, well, any idea what he's saying?" Samantha asked, a hint of desperation in her voice. "Because it sounds a lot like *I hate you* at three in the morning."

"He's trying to get used to the world," Serah said. "He's just so new to it all, you know? Completely helpless and innocent."

"You sound like the baby whisperer."

Serah laughed as a loud knock echoed through the house from the front door. The banging startled the baby, who started crying even harder. Samantha stood up and started for the door, but stalled beside Serah's chair.

"Can you, uh…?" She paused as whoever it was knocked again. "Can you hold him for a second?"

Before she could respond, the baby was thrust into her arms. Serah gripped hold of him, eyes wide, and stared down at his little body. Samantha let go, taking a step back, her hands up as if to make sure

Serah had him before she let her guard down.

Serah smiled, cradling him in one arm, as she stroked his cheek with a pointer finger. His skin felt electric, tingling her fingertip. He quieted down at her touch, his cries shifting to whimpers, seconds later stopping completely.

"Holy shit," Samantha said. "You *are* the baby whisperer."

The third knock was louder than the first two. Groaning, Samantha yelled for them to hold their horses as she strolled that way. Serah stared at the quiet baby as he peeked his eyes open and stared up at her. He was three weeks old today, and it was the first time Serah had held him or had even seen him any closer than crying in his mother's arms.

"Hello, Samuel," she whispered as she continued to stroke his warm cheek. "I'm Serah."

He just stared at her.

"Your parents are good people," she continued. "Your sister, too. Some of the best people I've ever met. You're a lucky little boy to have them, so you need to cut them some slack. Your mom could use a bit of sleep."

"Ugh." Samantha's voice rang out as she closed the front door again. "I swear, he's such an asshole."

"Who?"

"The landlord," she groaned. "He came to complain that the grass hasn't been mowed in like, a year. I told him Nicholas would get to it whenever he could. I mean, we have a newborn, and my husband is hardly ever at home... excuse the hell out of me for not making yard work a priority. I haven't slept in days."

"Why don't you sleep now?"

"Because Samuel's..." She hesitated. "...*not* crying. He's not crying. How did you do that?"

"I didn't do anything."

"Baby whisperer," she said again, smiling as she carefully picked Samuel back up. She watched him carefully, like she expected him to start crying again, but he remained quiet. "Oh God, Nicki doesn't get home from camp for a few hours. Maybe I can sleep. You think?"

Serah laughed. "I think."

Samantha mumbled apologies about not being better company, but Serah shrugged her off, hugging her friend before heading out the door.

She showered and ate an early dinner alone before heading out for work a few hours later. She walked, strolling along casually, her footsteps stalling when she neared the old motel and saw the familiar form standing right outside. "Luce?"

He turned, his eyes scanning her carefully. "Serah."

There was something in his voice, something she couldn't quite place. It was strained, like he was holding something in. She ran into him occasionally the past few weeks, but it had been a few days since she saw his face. Since their night together, he'd been keeping his distance.

As he stood there in front of her, she could tell his thoughts were far away. His eyes kept drifting over her head and all around her like he was looking for something. She glanced beside her, curious, but all that met her were the normal Chorizon streets.

Maybe he's just avoiding facing me...

"Are you okay?" she asked hesitantly.

"I'm fine."

"You seem... distracted."

He offered her a tentative smile. "You're not the only one who can sense things."

"What do you sense?"

"Something that shouldn't be here."

The way he looked at people as they passed, Serah suspected it was more of a 'someone' than a 'something'. She started to express that when Luce suddenly reached out, grabbing her. She tensed, surprised, but relaxed when he wrapped his arms around her. He smelled warm, like earth, a slight hint of sulfur on his skin.

Serah slipped her arms around his waist, hugging him as he pressed a kiss to the top of her head. The embrace didn't last long before he pulled away. "You should get to work before you're late."

"Yeah," she said, taking a step back, her eyes still on him. "Hey, Luce? Can you do me a favor?"

He hesitated. "What?"

"Can you maybe mow my neighbor's grass?" she asked. "Mine's taken care of by my landlord, but theirs... well, their landlord isn't as nice as mine."

He stared at her. "You want me to mow grass?"

"Yes," she said. "If you don't mind."

He didn't respond, but nodded slightly, the only answer she figured she was getting.

"And try to be quiet about it," she told him. "You know, since they have the baby and everything."

"Quiet," he said. "Got it."

She offered him a wave as she took another step away before turning and heading inside the lobby of the motel.

She paused when she reached the door, glancing back, but he was gone already.

Serah didn't much mind the nightshift, although it could be a little boring most of the time. Especially weekdays, like today, where very few people traveled through this town. They had two occupants, and nobody came into the lobby for hours.

It was dark outside, approaching midnight, as Serah sat beside the desk, reading a trashy little romance novel she'd plucked out of one of the drawers. She assumed it belonged to Gilda. She was skimming a particularly indecent scene, her cheeks flushing from the obscenity, when the door opened, the bell dinging. Serah anxiously closed the book, dropping it back into the drawer, and called out a "welcome" as she glanced up. The smile on her face melted, quickly wiping away when she realized nobody was there.

Her eyes looked around the lobby, confused. "Hello?"

"Hello."

The voice came from right behind her, so close the hair at her nape prickled, a chill shooting down her spine. Fear tensed her muscles as she spun around in the chair, coming face to face with a familiar man. It took her a few seconds in her alarm to recall his name. "Don."

He grinned. "You remember."

"Uh, yes," she said tentatively, standing up and edging away, stepping out into the lobby as the man lingered behind the desk. Bells and whistles went off in her head. Something wasn't right. Luce's earlier words rang through her mind. *Something that shouldn't be here.* "Can I help you?"

"As I said before, you can," he said, slowly stepping around the side of the desk. "You can help me in ways nobody else can."

This wasn't right. Serah's defenses prickled as her eyes darted around. It was so late, the town was dead at this hour, no one roaming or awake to hear her if she needed to scream. Serah counted to three in her head, her heart racing frantically, before she turned to run for the door, hearing his voice call out behind her. "Ah, don't be like that!"

She grabbed ahold of the door, the bell dinging above her as she ran out into the night, looking over her shoulder at the door to make sure he wasn't following. She swung back around just in enough time to collide with something, a scream bubbling up inside her. She looked up, scarcely making the man out in the pitch darkness as she stumbled backward, her knees nearly buckling.

"Why'd you go and run?" Don asked. "I wasn't going to hurt you."

"How...?" She stammered, shocked, glancing back at the building. He hadn't followed her out. She was certain of it. "You were just... and now you're..."

In a blink, he was gone from in front of her, suddenly twenty feet to the right before disappearing again, appearing right in front of her face just long enough for her to let out a sharp scream. Again and again, he flickered all around, vanishing right before her eyes. She spun around in a circle, terrified as he popped up all around her.

"This isn't real," she chanted, her voice unsteady as she came to a stop, his image vanishing and not reappearing, the parking lot still... so still... *too* still. There wasn't a breeze, not a cricket chirping, nothing. It was as if the world around her had hit pause. "It isn't real. It's can't be. This isn't happening."

"Oh, but it is."

The voice was barely a whisper as shadows fell over her, blocking out the small shred of light offered from the motel signs. Her breath hitched, her body shaking as she slowly turned around, coming face to face with the eerie figure. She cried out, terror gripping her insides. His sharp face was twisted angrily, despite his grin, his eyes dark pits of blackness. Blackness cloaked him, dark shadows surrounding him. It was Don, but it was something else now… something unnatural.

Something *not* human.

"Oh God," she cried. "What are you?"

"You know what I am," he said, "and I think it's time you remember."

Before she could react, before she could run, or scream, or beg for mercy, pray to God to save her, hands roughly grabbed ahold of her, blackness whisking her away.

Luce popped up in front of Serah's house.

It was pitch black out, an antique clock in a neighboring house chiming exactly midnight. The witching hour, they call it, the time where human folklore says witches, and demons, and ghosts are most powerful, where black magic is strongest, where the world is most dangerous.

What people don't seem to realize, though, is it's

always dangerous. It's not just the supernatural world they have to contend with. When you're mortal, life is nothing more than a drawn-out game of Russian Roulette. Every moment is the spin of a gun cylinder, every decision pointing the barrel at your head. Over and over, again and again, you pull the trigger, hoping it won't be your last turn in the game.

Angels were blessed with knowing which would be the last, which decision would hold the bullet ending it all. Luce could look at every mortal and know when they would take their last breath and what would happen to their souls afterward with just a glance.

Luce knew their futures, but he didn't know Serah's. He should've been able to tell, when she opened her eyes in the street that day, what would come of her, but there was nothing. There was never anything. Every moment was like her last, until another moment happened, replacing the one before it. There was no life, no death, and no future, just a right now. A right now she'd been living for months. The muzzle of the gun was pressed to her temple but nobody had pulled the trigger yet.

Sighing, Luce looked away from her quiet house, turning to the neighbor's. He could feel Samuel's essence all over the place. His future was easy to see, a long and happy life before he ascended back to Heaven where his soul originated. Luce wished he could see that for Serah.

Fuck, he wished he could see *anything* for her.

If she was destined for Heaven, he could walk away, leave her in peace with a life he'd forced upon her. If she were destined for Hell, he would fight tooth and nail to save her. But she seemed to just be fated to exist in the moment. What would happen when her heart stopped beating?

He waved his hand toward the yard around the Barlow house. The grass shriveled, withering back into the ground until it was the same short length as everyone else's. He was watching it when a peculiar sting shot down his spine, a feeling that had consumed him all day.

It felt like a knife in his back.

Danger.

He searched out Serah, straining himself to sense her across town, and froze when he faintly caught the melody of her heartbeat. It thumped feverishly, so hard he could ear its echo like it was banging against her ribcage, desperately trying to escape. The second the sound struck him, another joined it, jarring him as the pop of static ricocheted through the neighborhood, so loud dogs started barking, a nearby car alarm suddenly wailing.

Luce turned, seeing a dozen angels, some with recognizable faces, a few with weapons but most unarmed. The brazen fuckers were visible, shields completely down. Any mortal could look out the window and see them descending upon the neighborhood. He scanned the crowd for Abaddon, but his old friend was nowhere to be found. Luce sought him out, uneasiness in the pit of his stomach.

Anger gripped him.

The Guardian was startlingly close to that frantic heartbeat.

The angels started toward Luce as he reached for his weapon, gripping it tightly. He had the advantage, since they couldn't take his wings, but they could wound him enough to keep him from leaving. Some of them faltered when he pulled his knife out, but one brave Power lunged right for him. They were slow, and sloppy, clearly not the best fighters up above. They weren't sent to stop him, or harm him. They were a deterrent.

A distraction.

That son of a bitch.

Luce swung his knife, stabbing, grabbing, slicing, dicing, and nicking every bit of angel he could reach. They swarmed him on all sides, Grace bathing him when he plunged his knife through an angel's chest and yanked it back out. He scarcely had time to enjoy the sensation, to relish in the surge of energy, when a knife stabbed him in the side. He grunted at the sharp pain, swinging toward his assailant, a pretty little Virtue in a red gown. *Pity.*

Luce grabbed her arm, twisting it, pulling the knife straight from her hand. He stabbed her with it, stabbed her straight in the stomach, bringing his own blade down through her back when she hunched over. She exploded in a ball of light, surrounding him, the tingle easing some of the burn from the wound.

Fuck, he hated how slow he healed.

"Michael," he shouted, looking up at the night sky as he fended off another attack, taking a nick to the cheek. "Brother, if there's ever a moment for you to try to intervene in my goddamned existence, this would be it."

He swung around, taking out the winged bastard that had cut him. Another female. He sliced another, swinging around as a second loud pop of static tore through the neighborhood.

Luce's eyes instantly met a pair of familiar ones. Michael.

"Thank fucking Heavens," Luce groaned.

"I'm not doing this for you," Michael said right away, swinging his sword, taking two out at once.

"I know you're not," Luce said. "I'm just glad you're doing it."

More static rocked the night, more angels appearing. "Reinforcements," Luce muttered. "Beautiful."

There was a pop of static directly to his left, not but a few feet away. He turned, about to throw his knife right at whoever it was, but hesitated with it raised. Another pretty Virtue, but this one he knew. *Hannah.*

"Not you, too, sunshine," he said. "Tell me you're not one of Abaddon's fools."

She froze, genuinely stunned by the sight, before her face twisted in disgust. "Never."

"Good to know," Luce said, shoving her out of the way to take out an angel behind her. "So what are you doing here?"

"Serah," she said, her voice urgent. "She's in trouble."

Luce nodded, swinging around, throwing his

knife halfway across the yard and impaling a burly looking Power right in the forehead. He flicked his wrist and his knife can hurling back, the angel exploding into a cloud of expelled Grace. He turned to Michael, seeing his brother was bogged down. It wasn't a matter of winning or losing. They'd win... no doubt about it. Archangels never lost. It was a matter of battle, of endurance, of taking out the other side.

Michael looked over at him, nodding. "Go."

"You sure about that?"

Just as he said it, another loud pop rocked the street, quaking the ground. More angels appeared, this time Powers sent from above. Luce laughed to himself. His Father had sent help.

"I am now," Michael said, turning his focus to Hannah. "You know how to use a knife, Virtue?"

Hannah nodded. "Samuel taught me long ago."

Michael tossed her a discarded weapon, and she caught it mid-air.

"Don't hold back," he told her. "They won't."

Luce didn't hesitate any more, zapping right out of there and to the old motel. The place was unlocked, the door open, lights on, but nobody was around. Her heartbeat was gone, as was Abaddon. He sought them out, zapping from place to place, city to city, and country to country, going everywhere he sensed Abaddon had gone, until finally... finally... he found him.

The Guardian stood on a ledge at the top of the Empire State Building, wings fully expanded, his eyes black as night. He had an arm wrapped around Serah's chest, his free hand clutching a knife. He held it to her throat as she trembled, tears streaking her flushed cheeks. She was barely holding herself together. Abaddon's strong grip was the only thing keeping her upright. "Ah, speak of the devil and he shall appear."

Serah cried loudly, letting out a horrified scream when Luce manifested in front of her. He froze in spot, a few feet away as his eyes met hers. He could feel her fear, the sensation so overwhelming that it nearly crippled him. He knew what she saw when she looked his way. His massive wings were fully expanded, the knife gripped firmly in his hand. Blood trickled down his cheek as more coated his ripped shirt on his side.

"I'm glad you could make it," Abaddon said, his voice calm. "Do me a favor and toss aside that knife, will you?"

Luce hesitated before dropping his knife. It

J.M. Darhower

clattered against the concrete of the ledge, landing between them. "What do you think you're doing, Don?"

"What I have to," Abaddon answered right away. "I didn't want it to come to this, but you gave me no choice."

"You've always had a choice," Luce said. "You chose to join me long ago, and then you chose to abandon me when it suited you. You chose to stand around while I was punished for your indiscretions. So don't talk to me about choices, because you have them, and you've made them. But now, old friend, you've severely limited mine."

A slow smile spread across his lips. "That's where you're wrong, Lucifer."

The second Abaddon said his name, he closed his eyes, hearing the gasp escape Serah's lips, a surprising exhale. "Lucifer?"

Abaddon laughed, looking genuinely amused when Luce opened his eyes again. Serah was staring at him, stunned. He could see she had questions, questions Abaddon, too, sensed.

"Aw, you didn't know, did you?" Abaddon asked, the words full of forced compassion that didn't at all match the amusement that danced in his eyes. "You

226

didn't know your lover was the one-and-only Lucifer. The elusive Prince of Darkness. Here he let you think he was some storybook Prince Charming when really he's the King of Hell."

Serah's lips parted, the next word barely a breath, but it held so much power it nearly knocked Lucifer off the ledge. "Satan."

Satan.

He hated that fucking name.

Abaddon tugged on Serah roughly, yanking on the fabric of her shirt with the hand snaked around her, exposing part of her chest. His fingertips traced her scar. His words were directed at Serah, but Luce knew they were meant for him, that they were meant to wound him in a way no knife would.

"Who do you think gave you this scar?" Abaddon asked as he pressed his palm against her chest. "Who do you think took your memories away?"

"No," she whispered, shaking her head. "No."

Luce couldn't meet her eyes. He knew she'd see the truth in his.

"You see, Serah," Abaddon said, "you were once like us. Once, not long ago, you had wings. But Lucifer here manipulated you. He robbed you of everything, left you bleeding in the street. And he did it all with that knife right there, the one laying in front of you on the concrete. You were innocent, until the notorious Lucifer tore you to pieces, one whispered lie at a time."

"Luce," she called out, her voice quivering. "Please tell me that's not true. Tell me this isn't real. Tell me something... please... tell me I'm crazy."

Luce met her eyes, drinking in the heartbreak those words had caused. That heart, a heart he savored every time it beat, was shattering over him. "You're not crazy. You've never been crazy."

"No," she whispered again. "Don't tell me that. Please. Don't... don't tell me this is real."

"I am who he says I am," Luce said. "I did what he says I did."

"No." She nearly collapsed as sobs tore through her. "Don't say that!"

"It's the truth," Luce continued, trying to ignore the ache her words caused. "I took half of the angels down with me when I fell, and I took you, too. I took you cruelly. You trusted me. You believed in me. You thought everyone was wrong when they called me Satan, but I proved them right by making you fall."

"You're crazy," she cried.

"No, I'm just a sinner," Luce said. "And a liar. And

a snake. I ruled Hell for six thousand years until you helped me escape."

She could do nothing but stare at him. Devastation marked her features. Defeat slumped her shoulders. Her tears steadily streamed down her cheeks, but he could do nothing to dry them when he'd been the one to cause them in the first place.

"I'm a lot of bad things, Serah, but that's not all I am, nor is that why we're here," Luce continued. "You see, there's something else I am, something Abaddon knows."

"What?" she asked. "What are you?"

"I'm in love with you," Luce said quietly. "He found my weakness."

Serah never had a chance to respond. Before the last syllable was from his lips, a painful gasp echoed through air as the knife Abaddon held sliced through Serah's throat. Blood streamed from the wound as he let go of her, shoving her right over the edge.

Make your choice, brother, and make it quick.

Abaddon's words rang through Luce's mind as he hesitated for a fraction of a second. A fraction of a section, barely a blip, but it was almost too long. He dove off the side of the building, soaring as fast as he could, snatching a hold of Serah just a second before she hit the ground.

Screams rang out all around, from people on the ground, the entire block seeming to come to a standstill to watch. Luce yanked her body into his arms, leaving mass hysteria in his wake as he apparated, vanishing into thin air.

He made his choice.

He chose Serah.

He left Abaddon alive on the ledge.

He didn't have another second to spare.

Luce popped back up in Chorizon, right in front of Serah's home. The chaos had dwindled, the rebel angels defeated thanks to Michael. The moment Luce appeared, Hannah rushed toward him, frantic, but his eyes were solely on his brother.

"Save her," he said. "I beg of you, Michael."

Michael stared at Luce, gaze drifting to Serah, limp and bleeding out in his arms. His eyes met Luce's once more. Seconds passed, long torturous seconds that were accented by Serah's fragile heartbeats.

He was squandering those seconds, wasting too much fucking time.

"Michael," he yelled. "Please!"

Michael looked away, and Luce knew it then. He wasn't going to do it. He wouldn't help him.

Not again.

Luce couldn't be surprised. He knew how it went. Serah was a mere mortal. Sooner or later, she'd die anyway. Since that day in the garden, they'd watched over a hundred billion perish.

She was just one life.

But she was important to him.

Lucifer felt drained, the energy seeping from his body as he clung to Serah. Dropping to his knees, he sat in the yard, staring down at her. Devastation rocked him, the one feeling that he'd never grow used to nagging at him. Remorse.

"I'll find Abaddon," Michael said, his voice strong and steady. No sympathy. "He'll pay for what he has done."

In an instant, Michael was gone, all hope whisked away with him. The other lingering angels slowly followed, leaving Lucifer alone.

Alone.

So fucking alone.

He still wasn't used to that.

"You're not alone."

The unexpected declaration tingled Luce's spine as it rang out just behind him. Luce closed his eyes as that voice washed through him.

When he opened his eyes again, He stood in front of him. His Father, in all His glory, stood on Earth's soil again. It had been a long time since He last ventured down here. A very long time.

"Since that afternoon in the Garden," He said, adding to Luce's thoughts. "That was the last time I came."

"Why are you here now?" Luce asked, a bitter edge to his voice he couldn't restrain. It came from a place deep down inside of him. "I'm not in the mood for an 'I told you so'. I'd rather be alone with her, to have a moment... just one more moment... before they take her."

A reaper hovered above. Luce hadn't looked up, probably couldn't even see it in the darkness if he did, but he could sense it lurking. He didn't want to consider what that meant at the moment. Reapers only delivered souls one place.

She didn't deserve that.

His Father looked up at the sky, staring for a moment before glancing back at Lucifer. "It's not here for her."

Lucifer met his eyes. "It's not?"

He shook His head. "A lot more angels fell tonight, Lucifer."

"So she's not..." Luce glanced back down at Serah.
So she's not going to Hell...

"No, she's not."

Lucifer closed his eyes, relief rushing through him as he absorbed that information. "I wasn't sure. I can't see her future. I've never been able to."

"I know," He said. "Nobody can. I've kept it to myself."

"Why?"

It was a question asked of Him often, but one He usually never answered. This time, though, He didn't ignore it. He offered Luce what he craved — the truth. "You two are so entwined it's difficult to distinguish where you end and she begins. Her future was never set because you hadn't decided yours. I gave you what you wanted, Lucifer. I allowed you free will. Every choice you made altered what happened to her."

Free will. It didn't quite feel as freeing as Luce thought it would.

"That's the thing about free will," He continued, once more reading Luce's thoughts. "Decisions have consequences. They don't just impact you, but everyone around you also. Every choice you made somehow altered what happened to her."

"So I did this," Luce said. "I destroyed her again."

J.M. Darhower

His Father stepped closer. "She's still breathing."

"For now."

"Yes, for now," He agreed. "So you have a decision to make, son, and it's not going to be easy."

"What is it?"

"Whether or not you want to keep your wings."

Lucifer stared at Him.

"You can keep them," He explained, "and I'll welcome you back home."

"And what? If I give them up, I get dragged back to the pit?"

"You get a second chance, Lucifer." His eyes turned to the Barlow residence. "Just like Samuel did. You'll have a true clean slate, something you asked for often the past few months, and not just from others. You get a clean slate from yourself, too."

"That's not an option," Luce said, brushing hair out of Serah's pale face. "I don't want to exist a single moment without remembering the sound of her heartbeat."

His Father nodded. "So wings it is."

Reaching out, God pressed a hand to Luce's forehead. Instantly, intense warmth filled him, consuming every inch of him. It was familiar, the sensation like a hit of a drug he'd tried to kick.

234

His Grace.

The moment his Father moved his hand, Lucifer pressed his own palm to Serah's chest. *Please don't be too late.* He channeled it, pushing it out of himself and into her. Her wounds mended, her body glowing radiantly as Lucifer healed her with his Grace.

Picking her up, he carried Serah inside the house, taking her back to the bedroom. He laid her down on the bed, her body limp, unconscious, but she'd wake up soon, feeling brand new.

"Forgive me," he whispered, "but you have to forget all this ever happened. You have to live this life not remembering me."

He kissed her forehead, standing up to leave, when the images flooded him, striking him so hard he stumbled. Serah. A long, happy life, full of love and friends, living just next door to her angelic brother, watching him grow, before succumbing to a peaceful death down the road. He stalled in the doorway, a smile forming on his lips.

Now *that* she deserved.

When he stepped outside, his Father still lingered.

"Thank you," Lucifer said, the words catching in his throat. He wasn't sure if he even managed to speak them out loud, but his Father heard.

"You're welcome." He turned as if He planned to leave but hesitated, motioning toward Lucifer. "Before you come home, consider doing something about your clothing."

Lucifer laughed. "Unless you call Moses back up and make 'thou shalt wear white' a commandment, there's not a chance in Hell you're going to get me back in that white suit."

Abaddon was on his knees, his head held high with pride, not an ounce of remorse inside of him. The end of Michael's blade of fire was pointed at the Guardian's chest, yet the angel showed no fear at all.

Michael was close to thrusting the sword in, close to taking Abaddon's wings, when the air behind him shifted, another angel appearing. The powerful familiarity struck Michael right away, without even looking. He knew that Grace. He knew it, because he shared it. *Impossible.*

Turning his head, he watched, stunned, as Lucifer strolled a few steps toward them. Definitely impossible, but yet it was so. His skin glowed, his body healed, the sins that had tainted him dulled to a minimum. They weren't completely wiped away, and they probably never would be, but he had his Grace again. He was keeping his wings.

"Michael," Lucifer said casually in greeting.

Satan was on the tip of his tongue, but he couldn't say it. He couldn't call him that. Satan didn't have Grace. Satan didn't have the same configuration as him.

He nodded after a moment. "Lucifer."

"Call me Luce."

Michael smiled at the way in which he said that. He had been the one to give him that nickname in the first place. "Luce."

"Touching," Abaddon grumbled. "If you two are finished, I'd like to get on with this. Do what you came to do, Prince."

Before Michael could make a move, Luce grasped him, his palm against his chest, pushing him away. "Allow me."

Michael retreated, lowering his sword. Lucifer had certainly earned the right to be the one to deliver Abaddon's punishment, but it concerned Michael heeding to him. It had been too long since he'd had to, too long since Lucifer held power anywhere but below the soil.

Michael pulled out the gold knife he'd found on Abaddon and tossed it to Lucifer. Catching the Heavenly blade, Lucifer stared at it in silence, a sudden smile overcoming his face that alarmed Michael.

Lucifer turned his focus on Abaddon, twirling the knife in his hand as he closed the distance between them.

Still, Abaddon showed no fear.

"How's your mortal?" Abaddon taunted.

Michael expected Lucifer to explode at the question, but he barely reacted. "She's alive."

"Interesting. She didn't look so well last I saw her." Abaddon's eyes shifted to Michael. "I'm curious how that happened."

Michael didn't respond. It hadn't been him.

"You always seem to be curious about *something*, Abaddon."

Abaddon shrugged casually. "Guilty."

"Guilty," Lucifer echoed. "That you certainly are… guilty as sin."

The tip of Lucifer's knife pressed against Abaddon's chest. The Guardian screamed as the blade dug in, burrowing through his skin.

"You're one to talk," Abaddon growled through

clenched teeth. "Where do you think I learned it all, huh? Who do you think taught me all my tricks?"

"You learned nothing from me," Lucifer said. "What I tried to teach you was strength, and respect, and loyalty... I tried to teach you to stand up for yourself, to fight for what was just, and fair... but all you know, Don, is cowardice. All you know is evil. You stood up for self-interest, not for justice, and that's not the lesson I aspired to teach."

Abaddon glared at Lucifer, his dark eyes burning redder as he howled again when Lucifer twisted the blade of his knife, digging it in a little deeper. Michael considered stopping him, to put a halt to what Lucifer was doing. They weren't in the business of torture. This was supposed to be about punishment. But Lucifer's calm expression kept him from intervening. This wasn't done with sinister intent. This was just the Archangel's brand of penance. His eyes were pure, as bright blue as the afternoon sky had been before the reapers had surrounded the area, blanketing the sky in the sort of darkness usually only brought upon by night.

"You are an enemy to humanity," Lucifer said, his voice quieter than Michael had ever heard it before. "You show no remorse for anything. Repent, Don, before it's too late. Ask for mercy, and I'll show you it."

"Never."

For a moment, a short moment, it seemed as if the world had fallen still. Nobody moved. The air was devoid of sound. But as quick as it came upon them, it was shattered by the quiet, stoic voice. "I was hoping you'd say that."

A screech of agony echoed through the air as the blade of Lucifer's knife sliced through Abaddon's chest. It didn't puncture him, not going deep enough remove his wings, just scratching the surface and siphoning out what was left of his Grace. In the blink of an eye, the ancient sigil appeared, the star locked in a circle burned into the Guardian's chest.

The Mark of Satan.

Lucifer pulled the blade away, his eyes burning red. So, so red. It made Michael's spine prickle as his blade of fire ignited in response to the scene, when Lucifer kicked Abaddon hard, sending the angel skidding a few feet away on his back. Dropping the knife, Lucifer raised his hands defensively and turned to Michael before he could react. The smile was back on his lips, the red dulling as the reapers descended from the sky, Abaddon's wailing escalating as he was attacked by the black masses.

Reignite

"Sorry, brother," Lucifer said, the blue once more reappearing in his eyes. "Old habits die hard."

Michael was silent, pointing his sword at Lucifer, as he watched Abaddon be carried away. The sky cleared when the reapers disappeared, leaving the world around them in silence again.

Slowly, Michael lowered the blade. "He's gone."

"For now," Lucifer said, "but not forever."

"How do you know?"

"Because I'm here," Lucifer said. "I know what being in the pit does to you. Give him a few thousand years to get adequately pissed off and he'll find his way out of there."

"Then why did you send him there? Why not end him now?"

"Because when I take him out, brother, I don't want him to be on his knees," Lucifer said, picking up his knife and twirling it for a moment. Michael watched with fascination as Lucifer sliced his own hand with the blade. There was no blood, simply a line of glowing light as some Grace trickled out before the wound sealed. Lucifer stared down at it, smiling, before meeting Michael's eyes. "When I take him out, I want him to learn a lesson he was too dense to learn today."

"What's that?"

Lucifer stepped toward Michael, and he tensed, gripping the handle of his blade tighter, but he didn't move. Lucifer's smile grew when he caught it, though, his eyes flickering down to the sword briefly as he said, "Nobody fucks with an Archangel. *Nobody.*"

Michael shook his head as Lucifer laughed, the pop of static cutting off the amused sound as the Archangel disappeared. Michael stood there for a moment as something swam inside of him, something he tried to push back, but it got the best of him eventually: curiosity.

He apparated from the area and popped up in front of the small house in Chorizon. Serah was inside, fast asleep. Michael stood in the street for a moment, glancing around. All was how it had been the day before, the slate wiped clean, removing the fight between angels from all mortal memory. Michael remembered, though. He always would. Just like his brother, he remembered everything. He remembered how it felt the day he spared Serah not far away in the street, the grief he'd felt for the first time in his existence.

He'd felt it again, not long ago, right in this spot when he couldn't spare her again. Orders were orders, and his Father had expressly stated it when he'd been sent to help Lucifer.

Whatever comes of the one called Serah, you're not to intervene.

The grief of leaving her to die wasn't because of her lost life. It was because him and Lucifer were still connected, and he felt it inside of his brother, grief like he'd never known before.

Michael took a last look at the house before turning away. There was nothing left to make him want to stay. She'd left him long before today. Now it was time for him to let go.

Epilogue

Colors.

Mortals have thousands of names for them, different shades of different colors, only subtly altered from the one before it. They hold colors in high regard, mixing and matching, coordinating their clothing and painting their cars and even going so far as to alter the shade of their lawns. Colors, to them, are symbolic... they grow red with anger, they feel green with envy, or they catch the blues when they're feeling down.

It puzzled Lucifer.

Colors, technically speaking, are wavelengths of light. The eyes merely detect what light the item reflects most. There's nothing metaphorical about it. The shade the grass grows doesn't make it more or less useful. Pink tulips don't smell better than purple ones. If they put stock in reflected light, they should cherish white, as it reflects the most, whereas black simply absorbs it.

It's why angels are usually seen in white,

especially the Archangels. Light surrounds them. They're pure. It's also why Lucifer stood in the middle of a the vast white space he'd once again come to think of as 'home', wearing his usual get-up of black from head to toe.

Sixty years.

He'd stayed up here for the past sixty years, not stepping foot down below, and merely watched as the Earth continued to turn. It spun round and round, reflecting light, sustaining life, still the magnificent creation his Father dreamed it would be.

"Feels like just yesterday, doesn't it?"

Lucifer turned his head at the sound of the familiar voice, seeing Michael standing behind him. He saw his brother occasionally, once a month or so. Michael still spent most of his time in the throne room at their Father's side. Lucifer hadn't stepped foot in there since arriving, not because he wasn't invited... mostly because he felt like he didn't quite belong.

Maybe in another sixty years.

Only God knows...

"Feels like just yesterday you and I sat here," Michael continued, "watching the first human take their first breath."

"It practically was just yesterday,"

Luce responded, turning away as Michael took a few steps forward, pausing at his side.

Michael nodded, looking straight ahead at the image projected, the same image that had been playing in this spot for decades. Serah lay in a bed, just as she had last time Lucifer saw her in the flesh, only much older now.

"It won't be long," Michael said.

Lucifer whispered, "I know."

Her heart had beat almost two billion times since he'd left her. He'd counted every single one. And he knew she had only a hundred left before it wouldn't beat anymore.

Ninety-nine...

Ninety-eight...

Ninety-seven...

"You shouldn't be worried," Michael said. "What's mean to be—"

"Will be," Lucifer grumbled. "To everything there is a season, *blah blah* fucking *blah*, the wheel in the sky keeps on turning. You're wasting your breath, brother. I've heard it all before."

Instead of being annoyed, Michael smiled. The sight of it made Lucifer roll his eyes. He wanted to knock that grin right off of his *holier than thou* face.

Seventy-four...

Seventy-three...

Seventy-two...

"It's the truth," Michael said.

"It's bullshit," Lucifer countered, motioning with his head in the general direction of the throne room. "He knows what will happen, but the rest of us are in the dark."

"I don't think He knows."

"Again," Lucifer said, "Bullshit."

"I'm serious," Michael said. "Heaven is an idea. He doesn't create it. They create it. They spend eternity wherever they're happiest, wherever their souls are at ease. She was once like us, brother, but she has free will now. She will go where her soul chooses to be."

Forty-six...

Forty-five...

Forty-four...

Lucifer stared at the image, watching as her heartbeat slowed, growing weaker, inconsistent. He knew she wouldn't feel it when the end came. She'd go peacefully in her sleep. She never married, never had children, but she found a family in her friends. She became a teacher, led Sunday School at a local church, and volunteered her time to help others.

She was the definition of pure, her soul untainted and marked straight for Heaven.

But he had no idea where she'd go once she got here.

No idea who she'd be, or what she would see.

No idea if she would even remember him.

Twenty...

Nineteen...

Eighteen...

"Love bears all things, believes all things, hopes all things, endures all things," Michael said. "Love never ends."

Lucifer normally mocked his brother for quoting scripture, but he didn't have it in him at the moment. He found solace in those words, even if he wasn't sure what to make of them. "Do you think she loves me? I know I love her, but..."

But she'd never said it to him.

Had he done anything to really deserve her love?

He didn't think so.

"I suppose we'll find out," Michael said, once more giving him a smile before disappearing.

Lucifer stared at the image of her once he was alone before closing his eyes, focusing solely on the sound of her heart.

Three...

Two...

One...

The silence that met him then was deafening. His chest tightened. He squeezed his eyes shut tighter, feeling for her essence around him. He sensed it appearing, not far away, and channeled himself to that space.

To her Heaven.

Slowly, he opened his eyes.

A playground.

He knew the place. He'd been there before a few times, and he'd watched Serah go there nearly every day over the years. Chorizon Elementary School. All was quiet, only a soft breeze wafting through the playground. After a moment a squeak echoed through the air, the grinding of a rusty metal chain. Lucifer turned toward the swing set and froze when he saw her. She was so much younger than she'd been in recent years, utterly beautiful, wearing a peach dress, her long brown hair cascading around her shoulders. Bare feet drug the ground as she swung back and forth slightly, toes digging into the dirt. Her left hand clutched the chain, while in her right she held a familiar plant stalk.

Spider flower.

"You were right." Her voice was soft as she spoke, glancing away from the plant, looking toward him. "These flowers really do stink."

The pressure in Lucifer's chest lessened.

After a moment, she held it out, silently offering it to him.

He shook his head. "I can't smell anymore."

"I figured," she said. "That means there's nobody more perfect than you to give it to."

Lucifer laughed lightly, stepping toward her, carefully taking the flower from her hand. He stared down at it for a moment before meeting her eyes again. Neither said anything. Lucifer wasn't sure what to say. He'd survived six thousand years in Hell, but the past sixty without her were the most torturous of his existence.

"I didn't think..." he started. "I didn't expect..."

"Didn't expect what?"

"You to remember me," he admitted. "I did you wrong, Serah. I stole everything from you. I hurt you. I thought I'd show up here, and you wouldn't see me, because I wouldn't exist in your eternity... that Heaven, to you, would be somewhere I couldn't be."

She stared at him for a moment before her

expression softened. She swung for a second longer before standing up and stepping toward him. "I never forgot you, Luce. Even when I didn't know you, you haunted my dreams. My first thought, when I opened my eyes and found myself sitting on this swing, when I remembered every second I'd ever existed, was that someone had gotten it wrong, because this wasn't where I wanted to be."

"It wasn't?"

"No."

The air was disturbed around them before she could elaborate, loud pops as others apparated into the area. Serah turned away from him in just enough time for Hannah to descend upon her, grabbing her friend in an excited hug as Michael's voice cut through the air.

"Serah," he said, sounding about as nervous as he'd told Lucifer not to feel.

Serah pulled away from Hannah to look at him, smiling kindly. "Michael."

Before either could say anymore, another loud pop rocked the area. They all turned, and Lucifer froze when Samuel appeared in all his angelic glory. His mortal body had died months ago, appearing in Heaven back in his true form. Lucifer had avoided him, and Samuel hadn't sought him out. It was the first time they'd come face to face since the day he'd visited him at the gate so many years ago.

Serah gasped, rushing right at her brother. He picked her up, swinging her around in a circle as he hugged her tightly. "Told you," he whispered to her, just loud enough for Lucifer to hear. "I knew we'd have so many wonderful moments to come."

Serah smiled, clinging to him, before Hannah pulled her away again. Samuel greeted Michael casually with a slap on the back and turned to Lucifer, nodding, before once more stealing his sister back away. They vied for her attention, and Lucifer backed away, quietly giving them space. He turned to leave when arms suddenly wrapped around him from behind, stalling him. Sighing, he closed his eyes, taking a moment to savor her touch. "Angel."

"Luce."

He pulled her into his arms as he whispered, "I love you."

"I love you, too," Serah said, clinging to him. "When I opened my eyes, I didn't want to be here, because I didn't think you'd be here. I thought you'd be down there again, back in the pit, and I'd take an eternity in your Hell before I took a single second in my Heaven without you."

Those words wiped away all his worry, all his doubt, leaving him with a warm glow beneath his skin. She loved him. She did.

He pulled back some, opening his eyes to stare down at her. Her cheeks were flushed pink, her eyes sparkling brown with specks of a greenish hue. Shades of peach and tan coated her, pale in places, freckled in others. Her lips were naturally cherry red.

Leaning down, he softly kissed her.

He'd never appreciated color so much before...

Acknowledgements

Over a year ago, when I published Extinguish, I expected that to be the end. I felt like their story had been told, that what happened from there should be left to the reader's imagination. With a character like Lucifer, I didn't think he needed perfect bows or continuations. However, where Luce is concerned, things rarely go according to plan. He said fuck that, take this down... so I did, and here we are.

I want to thank everyone... yes, every single one of you reading this... for giving this story a chance. I knew it was risky, and I might fall flat on my face, writing about characters like Lucifer and Michael and their Heavenly Father, so I'm eternally grateful to everyone who took a chance on Luce and Serah. It wasn't always pretty and I know it isn't a "traditional" romance, but I hope you found their story worth it.

Many thanks to Sarah Anderson, as usual, for always listening to my ideas and reading my words and being both a championing and critiquing, for cheering me on but not being afraid to tell me when something sucks.

To my amazing family, who doesn't bat an eyelash when I tell them I wrote a story where Lucifer becomes the hero, and to my beautiful best friend, Nicki Bullard, for being so supportive every step of the way. You can always tell when I'm getting in a funk and know how to pull me out.